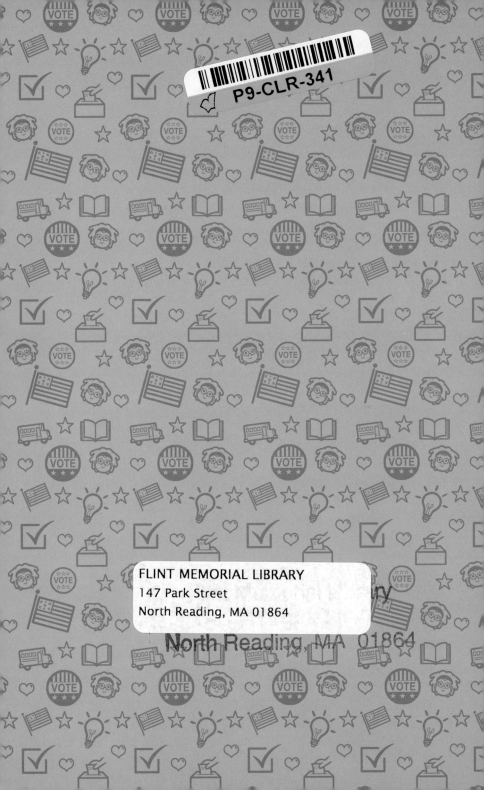

HOPE

Project Class President

HOPE

Project Class President

By Alyssa Milano
with Debbie Rigaud

ILLUSTRATED BY ERIC S. KEYES

Scholastic Inc.

Library of Congress Cataloging-in-Publication Data available

ISBN 978-1-338-32942-1

1 2020

Printed in U.S.A.   23

First printing 2020
Book design by Katie Fitch

Milo, Bella, Luke, Dorothy, Alice, Mary,
Claire, Annie, William, Anthony, and George.
You give me hope. I love you all so much.
—A.M.

For Xavier and Zora.
—D.R.

To my wife Jenni and her first year voting
as a US citizen.
—E.K.

HOPE

Project Class President

Chapter 1

"**H**ere they come!" I gasp and press my nose against the window of one of the double doors of the school's side entrance. In an instant, my mouth goes crackly dry, and I forget everything I want to say. *Think. Think!* "Um, hi, I'm Hope Roberts," I practice under my breath. "And I'm running for sixth-grade class president."

I watch the gleaming row of school buses pull up to JFK Middle. There's about eight of them—the last of which puffs out black smoke when it comes to a stop.

"Ew," I say, wrinkling my nose and momentarily aching for the environment.

Any minute now, the students pouring out of those buses—especially the sixth graders—will notice my sidewalk chalk arrows pointing them to the entrance by the sixth-grade lockers.

I grip the bar on the door and continue rehearsing. "I believe each of us has a unique role at JFK Middle, and as class president, I want to support you in yours."

A few students start down the path to this entrance. They look shocked they can come in this way. It's always locked! Grace calls it a crowd control thing, like how the science museum's entrances are set up. It took days of convincing the vice principal (and watering her many office plants), but Ms. Reimer finally approved my request to open them up.

"Just for one day," she said firmly.

Satisfied with my speech, I inspect my red sidewalk chalk lettering marking the shortcut to the sixth-grade lockers—courtesy of my new candidacy, of course. It reads: *6th Graders, Go a New Way* and *Go Hope Roberts for 6th Grade President.*

This is it—my official campaign launch! I want to make a difference at JFK Middle, and running for class president is a great way to do it. Thankfully,

my friend Grace has been helping me collect the signatures I need to get on the ballot. In fact, she's outside right now. I can imagine her at the carpool drop-off, petition in hand, directing sixth-grade foot traffic my way, like the amazing campaign manager she is.

In the week since I've decided to run, Grace has used her super-organized mind and famous spreadsheets to make sure we kick off this campaign strong. She helped me plan this launch to the detail, and so far, so great! It's still early in the campaign—election day is a month away—but some other candidates kicked off their campaigns a week before I did.

I study the campus activity while I wait for the crowd to notice the newly unlocked doors. Not long ago, this place was super unfamiliar, and a little bit scary. The ginormous fake tiger in the entryway seemed friendlier than half the kids wandering the halls. But I'm starting to get the hang of sixth grade. Science club is going great. My new friends Camila, Grace, and Henry are awesome. I've even gotten used to not sharing classes with my best friend, Sam. Sam's friends—Lacy, Golda, and Charlie—are now my friends, too. Just like my mom and older sister, I'm learning to carve out my very own place here. And even though I wouldn't have guessed it, I'm doing this by running for class president.

By the look of things, my campaign announcement is finally grabbing people's attention. The younger bus riders point to the arrows at their feet, break off from the crowd, and file in my direction. I get back in position, right next to my tall pile of campaign flyers set up on a stool in the middle of the sixth-grade lockers hallway. Sign-up clipboard in hand, I stand at attention, just like my comic book hero Galaxy Girl on the cover of issue 23. My feet are set apart and my cape-ready shoulders are pulled back. I want to look presidential, and I think I've nailed it.

With seconds to spare, I play out the entire scene in my mind. The sixth graders will be so pumped they get to use this entrance, they'll cheer when they see me and happily add their signatures to my list. I'll confidently introduce myself to a ton of kids I don't know, without feeling nervous at all. In no time, I'll collect the support needed to get on the

school ballot. The golden number is fifty signatures, and if I count my friends' signatures—which I keep safe in my back pocket—I only need thirty-nine more. *I've got this.*

The loud voices get closer. I even catch glimpses of the kids leading the pack. It's the moment of truth.

But as the double doors swing open, a gust of wind blasts through the long hallway, sending all my flyers . . . flying. Panicked, I drop my clipboard and start grabbing at the swirling paper that's now everywhere. I cringe as a few loose sheets smack people in the face. *Oh no!*

I'm a future astrophysicist and daughter of a

NASA scientist. *How* did I miss that the door at the other end of the hall is pinned wide open? These are the perfect conditions for a classic wind tunnel.

Now instead of cheers, a ripple of laughter breaks out. I can imagine what a wacky sight I am. I must look like one of those game show contestants in a money grab chamber. Except I'm not at all feeling happy or lucky—just majorly embarrassed. Try as I might, I can't block out the giggles or the comments.

But wait . . .

"Ha ha, awesome!" erupts one kid.

. . . is that an entirely bad thing? I listen closer.

"How cool is this?" shouts another.

Everyone sounds more giddy than mocking. Before I know it, people are grabbing flyers for me.

"Nice! Our very own sixth-grade entrance," one girl tells me as she hands over a neat stack of flyers.

"Thanks for your help, everybody," I say, taking all but one flyer from her.

"No prob," says a boy. "Thanks for making sixth graders feel like VIPs for once."

"I hope it gives you a Monday mood boost." I smile back.

Seeing everyone happy makes me happy. It's amazing noticing everyone holding their heads a little bit higher as they head off to class. The energy in this hallway is dialed up to one hundred.

It's then that I remember the golden number fifty. *The signatures! My clipboard!*

With my flyer-free hand, I scoop up the clipboard I'd thrown to the floor and place it on the now-empty stool. Thankfully, the last person from the buses has entered the building, so indoor weather conditions are no longer as breezy.

"I—I'm Hope Roberts, and I'm running for sixth-grade class president," I announce in a frenzy, trying to capture the kids who haven't left yet. "I'm collecting signatures so I can qualify to have my name added to the ballot. Will you sign my petition?"

"Sure!" says a girl I recognize from Spanish class. A few of her friends follow her to the pen I'm holding out.

Soon, my friend and campaign manager Grace is at my side, handing people a second clipboard.

"You're rating with carpoolers," she reports with wide eyes. "I got about fifteen signatures out there."

"Wow, that's amazing!" I'm so grateful, but I stop short of giving Grace a bear hug.

"Boy, people sure are in a great mood today," says Grace.

"It's the VIP treatment," I tell her.

"If we can keep them this happy, they won't forget you at election time."

"Fingers crossed," I say with a wink.

When the area has finally cleared, the high five Grace and I give each other echoes through the halls.

There's barely enough time to count the signatures before the late bell rings. Grace is quick at checking there are no name repeats. I hold my breath as she counts the last of the names.

"We're still missing six names," she says with a frown.

A crackle cuts through the sad silence, alerting me to the crinkling sheet of signatures stashed in my back pocket. *I'd completely forgotten about it!*

Hopeful, I snatch out and unfold the paper.

"Well, what're you waiting for?" Grace bounces on the balls of her feet, trying to get a peek. "Count 'em!"

". . . eight, nine, ten, eleven!" I rattle off breathlessly. "We did it!"

Grace and I can't stop Cheshire-cat grinning as we zip down the hall to class. I want to hold up my arms like a sprinter crossing the finish line, but a sobering thought stops me.

Sure, it's a huge deal I've scored enough signatures to get on the ballot. But why do I have the nagging feeling that this step may be the easiest part of this whole election process?

Chapter 2

The next morning, Grace stands beaming next to a posted list in the sixth-grade hallway. She's waiting for me to join her.

"There it is, in black and white for all to see," squeals my best friend, Sam, who gets there a few paces before me. Her outstretched arm gestures to the list. I huddle around with my friends to take a closer look. It's the list of the official candidates for sixth-grade class president.

My name is one of them! The other two are Naomi Francois and Mason Taylor.

Sam's hands make a flourish at me like I'm a famous painting at the Louvre. "There is no other

candidate more perfectly suited for the role," she says theatrically.

Fun and kinda cool fact: The closer we get to opening night of the school's upcoming musical, the more expressive Sam is. We're talking louder speaking voice, sharper enunciation, taller posture. And you know what? I honestly like that about her. It's mesmerizing watching her treat the world like a stage.

"Watch out, JFK Middle!" Sam bellows and throws an arm around me. "My best friend, Hope Roberts, is going to show everyone what sixth graders are made of."

"Woo-hoo! Go, Hope!" cheers Lacy, Sam's theater

friend. Lacy Torrisi never misses a chance to hype someone up.

I hug Sam and Lacy back. "Aw, thanks, you guys."

"Congrats, you two!" Camila says to me and Grace. She pulls out her phone and angles it for a group selfie. "Hold it right there—I'm jumping in!"

We snap a few fun pics, and Camila texts the best ones to our group chat.

Just then a group of people shuffle by and take notice of the list.

"Hope?" a baby-faced boy with a bored expression calls out to me. My opponent, Mason Taylor. I nod. I haven't met him before, but I recognize his face from

the amazing self-portrait on his campaign posters. "Congrats," he tells me.

I congratulate him, too, and we shake hands as if we're two awkward adults before he moves on.

A bigger crowd is forming around the list now.

"Wave or shake a hand." Grace nudges me. "You're now campaigning as an official candidate."

Whoa. That does sound like a major change from just collecting signatures. But somehow, I don't feel any different. That is, until Grace smiles and points her head in the direction of a small group of girls hanging around a nearby locker. "Psst . . . potential votes, twelve o'clock."

"You got this," says Lacy with her signature encouragement.

I made a speech at the science competition. I spoke at a town hall meeting when I was trying to save the animal shelter. Talking to a couple of sixth graders shouldn't be that much harder—right?

I thank my friends and watch them go in separate ways. I linger by the poster a little longer while I decide my first campaign move.

"It's going to be so exciting," says one of the girls to two friends leaning on either side of her locker. She's referring to the paper in her hand. *Could that be one of my flyers from yesterday?*

The friend on the right nods. "I think it'll be good for the school."

It's cool to hear students in support of the election process. Here's my chance to earn their votes while they're on the topic. I can just walk up and introduce myself as a presidential hopeful.

Galaxy Girl stance activated! I lengthen my spine, take a deep breath, and approach them.

"Hi," I greet them, beaming.

Three sets of questioning eyes look at me. But I get no greeting in return. There's just this heavy silence as they wait for me to state the purpose of interrupting them.

I guess they don't recognize me by my face yet.

Maybe if I let them know I'm Hope the candidate. "Uh, I noticed you talking about my flyer," I start.

"Are you in the musical?" the girl says.

"Uh, n-no," I say, caught off guard. *I guess I had the wrong flyer.* "It'll be super exciting, though. My friends Sam and Lacy are in the show. I can't wait to see it."

I'm rambling. All honest feelings, but I need to hit the brakes. My mouth is running on empty, and all raised eyebrows and confused stares are directed toward me.

Good thing I see someone I know.

"Hope to catch you there opening night," I say, waving goodbye and finally putting them out of their misery.

"Henry!" I say to the boy heading my way.

His eyes light up. "Hey, Hope."

"What's a seventh grader doing in these parts?" I ask, grateful for the distraction. And seeing Henry is my favorite kind of distraction. He's just so—er, nice to be around. As a friend. Totally, as a friend.

"I'm actually here looking for you," he admits.

My face tingles a bit, and I grin before I can stop myself. "Oh, really?"

We walk in the direction of my next class.

"Yeah, to congratulate you. I just heard the news you're running for class president."

My smirk cracks open to an all-out smile. "Thanks, Henry."

That's so sweet of him. It's nice how we're starting to hang outside of science club more and more.

"Henry, my dude, how are you?" a boy calls out to us.

I recognize the friendly face from the first time I crossed paths with him a couple weeks ago. He's the seventh grader with the elaborate handshakes—and he's running for student council vice president!

He and Henry go into their double backhand slap, side fist bump, and snap handshake.

"All good," answers Henry with a carefree nod. "Milo, this is Hope, from my science club. She's a newly minted candidate for sixth-grade class president," he adds proudly.

"Hope Roberts, yeah. I saw the list." His eyes

light up like he's genuinely happy for me. "Congrats to you!"

Milo high-fives me, then holds on to my fingers a second more before he slides away from them with a bouncy snap. I find myself bouncy snapping, too, as I finish the handshake a beat after him. I guess Milo and I just solidified our own official handshake. It's like this boy has a unique one with every single person. How does he even keep track? Making people feel special must be his superpower.

"Thanks." I grin, pumped up by Milo's friendly vibes. "I'm excited to be running."

"I am, too," Milo says, his supportive smile making it clear he's talking about his excitement over *my* campaign, not his. "Anyone who can work so hard to find homes for rescue animals is someone I can get behind."

"You know about that?" I ask, caught off guard. I didn't expect Milo to know anything about me.

He nods. "It was a pretty big deal."

"Wow, thanks so much." I bounce on the balls of my feet, surprised that the news about my work for the shelter had spread so much. "That was a total group effort," I say, twisting to face Henry. "Right, Henry?"

He gives a bashful smile back, smoothing down the front of his basketball jersey. I could swear I see the tips of his ears go red.

Before we realize it, a group of sixth graders walk over to greet Milo. Now that I've officially met the guy, I totally get why people flock to him and his friendly vibes.

"Hey, Mr. Soon-to-Be-VP!" one of them calls out, rapper style.

A grinning Milo answers back without missing a beat. "What about you, Miss MVP? Epic game yesterday!" He waves goodbye to me and Henry and goes to join the other group.

Henry and I don't hear the girl's response, but we grin when we hear the group erupt in a mini celebration of her athletic skills. I guess Milo's managed to turn the tables and share his spotlight, the same way he did with me just now.

"Did you meet Milo here at JFK?" I ask Henry after we take a few more paces.

"We're neighbors, so we hung out a lot growing up," says Henry. "I think he'll be great on student council, so I'm helping out with his campaign."

Who can blame Henry for joining Milo's team? It's easy to see how a candidate like that could boost JFK's school spirit. I would help Milo's campaign, too, if I weren't already busy with mine.

"Is he always so positive?" I ask, weaving through the foot traffic in the hall.

"I guess. That's just his personality," Henry calls out over the head of the person who's darting between us in the opposite direction.

"Is he like a performer or something? Because he

has a way with people," I wonder out loud. "He's gotta be in the musical, right?"

"Uh, no, he isn't."

I tap a finger to my chin as Henry and I return to walking side by side. "It's just that he's so—" I can't find the right term for "school-spirit-y," so I flutter my fingers and take bouncy steps instead.

There's an awkward silence coming from Henry's end. Just as I steal a glance at him, he speaks up.

"Um, do you . . . *like* him or something?" Henry asks through a frown.

I pump my fist. "Yes!"

Horror twists Henry's face, and I can't think what's gotten him so spooked. I mean, he's on Milo's campaign team.

"Don't *you* like him as a candidate?" I ask, confused.

With that question, the lines on Henry's forehead smooth out a bit. "Oh . . . yeah, of course."

I chuckle, relieved. "So why did you look so freaked out just now?"

Someone passes between us, and I can barely hear Henry shout, "I better go. My class is that way—see ya."

Before I can even respond, he lets himself get swallowed up by the crowd and disappears down a busy corridor.

Huh? I wonder if it was something I said.

Chapter 3

The printer in my parents' home office has been working so hard around the clock, it's starting to groan.

Our shaggy little dog, Cosmo, gives a whimper along with it.

"Stop being so dramatic." I giggle, scratching behind his ear.

"Let me guess—more flyers?" Mom asks. She's hanging new artwork next to the bookshelf and just dispatched Dad to grab her special tools from the garage. I'm sad to see the old painting go, but this one is even nicer. When your mom owns an art gallery, you don't get too attached to one piece of artwork.

I blow a wandering puff of curls out of my face. "Yup, more flyers."

Mom's soft chuckle gets muffled by another one of Cosmo's whimpers. Our other dog, Rocket, bounds into the room to investigate what all the racket is about. Satisfied no one is injured, she yawns and plops her large body down . . . right on my feet! I think she likes the feel of my fuzzy house slippers.

"Really, Rocket?"

Cosmo can't resist a good cuddle, so he trots over and nuzzles on top of his big buddy. Mom and I crack up.

"Now you, too, Cosmo?" I sputter, wobbling. My

flapping, stretched-out arms are barely keeping me balanced. "Okay, everybody up!"

When they still don't budge, I slowly pull my feet out of my slippers for a clean getaway.

Happily barefoot, I pad closer to the cranky printer to grab warm sheets of paper. I do one of Sam's fancy hand flourishes to show my mom.

"I love a smart, eye-catching flyer!" Mom says, giving me a thumbs up.

"Thanks." I smile. "I figure it'll be tons less awkward walking up to kids I don't know when I have something to hand them."

Mom's dark brown eyes peer over the old painting she's carrying across the room. "You've got this, sweetie," she huffs. "You've made speeches before, so I know you'll be fine talking to smaller groups."

"Yeah, but this is different," I answer, stuffing more flyers into the sleeves of my folder. "It feels normal getting people to care about a science project or a good cause. Asking strangers or people I barely know to be interested in *me* does not."

"Well, it's a good thing *you*, Miss Roberts, are an interesting person."

I make a face. "Um, I think you have the wrong Roberts. You and Marie are the charmers in the family. You two make friends faster than it takes Rocket to sniff out the secret stash of doggy treats."

"You're either born with it, or you're not," my older sister, Marie, singsongs as she traipses down the hall outside the office, cell phone in hand as usual.

Mom swats at the air like I have nothing to worry about. "Your sister is just teasing; that's not true."

I wait to hear Marie's bedroom door slam before I continue.

"Oh no? She graduated from my school last year, and people are still asking about her. And some kids can't even remember who I am week to week." I bust out my kooky *Can you believe that?* face.

Mom grins at my silly expression. "Stop exaggerating!"

Dad is back with Mom's tool kit and a handful of popcorn. He clearly made a detour through the kitchen. "What did I miss?" he asks, passing the small case to Mom.

"Your daughter here seems to have forgotten her rock-star public-speaking skills."

I chuckle when Mom gives him my exact *Can you believe that?* face.

"Now who's exaggerating?" I ask her.

She winks at me. "Sweetie, all I'm saying is if you just focus on your goals and your passion, and less on what people think of you, you'll be fine."

"Best of luck to you, President Hope," Dad chimes in. "And remember we're always here if you need us."

I smile, feeling grateful. "Thanks, you guys."

"You can thank us by loading new paper in the

printer," says Mom, inspecting her colorful painting's position on the wall. "It's fresh out."

"Oops." I chuckle and start hunting down some paper.

♡ ☑ ☆

The next morning at school, Grace and I meet up in a study group room for a campaign planning meeting. At first, it was all hard-core number crunching, because Grace insisted we break down the sixth-grade student body into potential votes for each candidate. But lately we've been talking strategy, which to me is a lot more fun. And our meetings have just gotten cooler now that we've scored our first major victory.

"Okay, we started the week on an amazing note," says Grace. "The side entrance idea made a great impression on sixth graders. Let's just keep building on that momentum."

"Yay, team!"

"Now we move into the self-promotion phase," Grace announces. "It sounds kinda cheesy, but you need to do some meet and greets. Ready to get out there and introduce yourself to voters?"

"Uh, don't I look ready?" I ask, showing her my cringey face.

Grace chuckles. "You'll get the hang of it. Take Milo, who's running for student council, as an example. I don't think there's a person at JFK Middle who doesn't know his name or face."

"I know, right?" I sit up straighter. "I wish there was a book on how to work a crowd like he does."

"Media training can help you learn that," says Grace. After I give her a blank stare, she continues. "It teaches you how to speak to a crowd or a reporter or whoever, all while staying on message."

"That sounds kind of like what Sam did at her theater camp last summer," I recall.

I can almost see a beaming lightbulb floating over Grace's head. "Then Sam's the one we need to get to train you!"

"Let's do it," I say, already composing a text to my best friend. She responds a few seconds later. "Sam's on board!"

"Awesome," Grace says as she rummages through the backpack on the empty seat next to her. She pulls out a booklet with the JFK logo on the cover and slides it across the table to me. "One more thing: Familiarize yourself with our student government handbook."

"Cool, thanks," I say, checking out the table of contents. It lists all sorts of campaign-related info, including election rules and deadlines. I stuff it into my bag—making a mental note to read the handbook as soon as I have time—and then I feel around for the flyers I printed yesterday. "And I have something for you," I tell Grace. I was excited when Grace assigned me with this task. So excited that I *may* have gone a little overboard with it.

I lay out three small piles of flyers I made. The first features an Albert Einstein quote—"*Politics is more difficult than physics*"—along with his famous tongue-out photo, followed by *Make the smart choice: Vote Hope Roberts*; the second, a simple and clean design with the headline, *Use Your Voice to Make a Choice—Vote Hope Roberts*; and the third is a round flyer made to look like a campaign button featuring a retro cartoon Uncle Sam and the slogan *JFK Middle School Wants YOU to exercise your right to vote. Choose Hope Roberts!*

"I need help deciding which of these flyers I should post around school."

"Hmm . . . tough call." Grace's eyes scan each of them. "And we can't put all three out, because we have to keep your message consistent . . ."

Just then another student walks in.

"Oh, I thought I booked this space," the girl says, clutching a journal.

"Oops, you did," I say, checking the clock on the wall. "Sorry, we'll be out of your way."

"Hey, before we leave," Grace says to the girl, "I wonder if you have a second to help us out with

something? We're running a campaign for Hope here, and we can't decide which flyer to pass out."

Clever move by Grace. She loves polling voters and getting their feedback. All the better for her data.

The girl's large brown eyes scan the both of us and the three piles on the table. She shrugs one shoulder. "Sure."

"Thank you," says Grace, offering the girl a formal handshake. The girl sets down her bag and her journal. "Like I mentioned, this is Hope Roberts, and my name is Grace Sullivan."

The girl takes Grace's hand and firmly shakes it.

"Hi, Grace. Hi, Hope," she says with a kind smile. "I'm Chloe Farzan. Nice to meet you both."

A few seconds later, Chloe—who, to Grace's delight, confirms she's a sixth grader—already has answers for us.

"Well, I would eliminate this one," she says, pointing to the round flyer. "It's too preachy, and kids don't like to feel like they're getting a lecture."

"Good point." I remove that pile and put them back in my folder.

"The Einstein one is fun, but not everybody's into science. So I'd go with this one." She points to the *Use Your Voice* flyer. "It's to the point, and the design is easy to read from far away," continues Chloe.

That decides it. We go with the clean design. Super grateful for her help, we thank Chloe and leave the room with smiles on our faces.

"Where has JFK Middle been hiding this girl?" I ask Grace.

"Another reason why a sixth-grade appreciation campaign would be so important," says Grace. "There are so many stars in our year."

Just as Grace and I head our separate ways, I see Henry heading down the hall toward me. My tummy does a happy flop. Henry walks me to my classes now and then. I like that this is becoming our way of hanging out.

But before I can make my way over to him, Milo calls out from behind me. "Hey, Hope!" I turn to face Milo, and he goes right into that special handshake he made up for me. I hardly remember it and fumble along the way.

"Rescue any dogs today?" he asks me with a caring smile.

"Aw, not today." I smile, marveling at him. This guy is incredible. His memory and people skills are off the charts.

"Listen, gotta run. You keep being a hero," he says as he continues down the hall.

Watching Milo fly off with a purpose sparks something in me. I can't slack off. I need to stay hard at work on this campaign.

The flyers! No time like the present to hang a few up. I still have a few minutes before class.

I zip back around and almost smack right into Henry.

"Hey-I've-got-some-stuff-to-take-care-of-before-class," I say, my sentence sounding like one long word said really fast. "Catch you later!"

"Bye," he says under his breath.

I can feel Henry watching me speed-walk away. Maybe seeing me so inspired about my campaign will spark something for him, too.

Chapter 4

I know my sour expression is poutier than a fish in Lemon-Lime Lake, but I just can't help it.

"Look at this," I tell Grace and Camila before I drop myself into the cafeteria chair across from them.

My friends both lean in over their sandwiches to inspect the stack of papers in my hand.

"What, *more* new flyers?" asks Grace. "I thought we agreed yesterday to use the message Chloe helped us pick."

I shake the crumpled pages before setting them down on the table. The crinkly chorus momentarily drowns out the din of chatter around us. "These are

the same flyers. But get this—they were thrown out seconds after I handed them to people."

"Ew, you dug them out of the trash?" Camila grimaces and slides her lunch protectively toward her.

I come to my senses and move the papers to the floor, anchoring my backpack on top of them.

"Sorry, guys, it's just that knowing these are barely read before they're tossed kinda stings." I frown.

"I'm sure it does stink." Camila covers her nose.

"No, I said it *stings*." I give a sad chuckle. "And, by the way, why doesn't this school have at least two recycling bins on every floor? Most kids threw these in regular trash cans just so they wouldn't have to search for one."

"Good question," says Grace. Her eyes drift to the ceiling as if tallying the low number of recycling bins she's seen today. I make a mental note to find out the answer.

Camila hands me a mini bottle of hand sanitizer and gestures for me to use some. "Sorry about your flyers," she says sympathetically. "That's rough."

"Tell me about it," I say. Shoulders slumped, I snap open my hot lunch, and the sight of my cheese quesadilla makes me sit up.

"Don't take it personally," says Grace. "There're just so many flyers being pumped through school lately. There's the musical next week and all the different campaigns going on—president, VP, secretary, and treasurer for each grade *and* for student council, and even random roles like community outreach officer. Plus, don't forget JFK Spirit Day is in a couple weeks. Kids don't know what to do with all the handouts coming at them."

Just then a wayward paper airplane darts right into my fluffy hair.

Camila giggles. "Well, that's *one* thing you can do with them," she says.

Grace grabs the flyer before I get a chance to see if it's one of mine.

"For the record," Grace says when she returns from the recycling bin, "it was a flyer for Spirit Day."

I nod, remembering that JFK Spirit Day is the biggest campaign event before the election. Grace and I are going to have to come up with the biggest, coolest idea to attract voters to our booth. And there'll even be a town hall there, for kids to ask the candidates questions.

"You see?" Camila gives me a reassuring nudge. "I bet each candidate has a few paper airplane leaflets right now."

I nod, until I think of a person who does things differently. "Not Milo," I say, poking the air with my fork. "He's all about having real face time with people. And it's working; you can tell he's got everyone's vote."

Camila points at me. "That boy's saving trees," she says. "But he does have a few campaign posters on every floor. And they look amazing!"

"You shouldn't compare yourself to Milo so much," says Grace with a shrug. "He's just a super-outgoing kid who's working that to his advantage. But he's running for student council for the whole school. We need to focus on what sixth graders care about instead."

I sigh, trying not to think of Milo's effortless campaigning. Shaking off the nagging thought, I lean in to pay attention to what Grace has to say. I can tell it's something good. She's doing the same glasses-adjustment move she makes before she wows our science club with a hypothesis or comes up with a solid strategy.

Grace's eyebrows peek above the top of her frames. "Remember how super excited people were when they got to come in through the side entrance?" she asks.

"Everyone could *not* stop talking about it," Camila says. "Mr. Gillespie had to threaten our class with *no homework* if we didn't settle down."

I smile, remembering how pumped we all were. "That was a cool moment," I say. "Sixth graders felt like the most important group in the school for a day."

"Exactly," says Grace. "We need to give them more of those kinds of moments. Help them feel more appreciated around here."

She's so right!

"More reasons to smile equals more reasons to vote," Camila singsongs the goofiest made-up melody, and I grin.

"I'm on board with that." I sit up. "This school can use a little sixth-grade appreciation."

"Yes!" Grace slaps the table. "And we need to let everyone know that *you're* the candidate to give it to them."

"Sixth-grade appreciation or bust," Camila singsongs again.

This time I chuckle out loud. "The slogans just keep on coming with you," I tell her.

"Got anything we can print on a T-shirt?" Grace asks Camila.

Camila closes her eyes and touches her fingers to her temples, like she's about to get a psychic premonition. "Let's see, I gotta have something for Hope." Her eyes fling open. "Hey, that's it! Gotta Have Hope!"

I crack up and clap like a baby seal. "Ha! I love it!"

"That's perfect," Grace squeals. "And it'll look great on a tee."

Camila bows her head and makes a hand flourish gesture. "My work here is done."

"Not so fast," Grace teases. "We can't properly spoil sixth graders without giving them some of your tasty home-baked treats."

Camila holds up her hands. "Okay, okay, I'll do it." She grins, shaking her head.

Grace and I cheer and thank Camila.

"And, Hope, do you think you can get your sister to make a few campaign tees we can wear to school?"

Marie's fashion design skills are legendary. And the cool thing is, Marie always has my back, even if she has a funny way of showing it sometimes.

"I'll ask her," I say. "I'm sure she'll want to help out."

"Great, looks like we've got Operation Sixth-Grade Appreciation covered."

Almost. Sweet treats and fun fashion may catch kids' attention, but if I want to keep it, I'll have to learn to make as good of an impression as Milo does. That's why I can't wait to start my media training with Sam after school.

We leave the cafeteria pumped about our campaign plans and our catchy slogan. And soon, I'll have public speaking under control with crowd-pleasing tips from a theater star. Then I'll be ready to *really* step up my game!

Gotta Have Charm. Gotta Have Confidence. Gotta Have Votes!

Chapter 5

After school, I make a beeline for the auditorium, where Sam is rehearsing for the musical.

"Don't move!" a man's voice booms from stage right. I freeze in my tracks somewhere between row M and row N. I barely breathe for fear of disrupting rehearsals even more. Everyone onstage is looking in my direction, and I want to liquefy until there are only two human puddles left—one in my right shoe, and one in my left.

"Perfect. Blocking complete."

Whew. The director is blocking the actors— theater-speak for positioning folks in assigned

places—not calling me out. I sigh in relief and sneak into the closest seat.

Thanks to Sam, I know more about theater lingo than I used to. When we were smaller, her mom would take us to local theater productions of different musicals.

At first I used to think they went on a bit too long. Now I can easily get lost in a show. My favorite ones are, of course, the ones Sam stars in. I've seen her in a few shows now, but this is her first one on the JFK Middle stage. Sam worked hard at theater camp over the summer to get ready for auditions. I was so happy when she and Lacy got cast in the show.

It's cool to see Henry work his magic for the musical, too. Aside from having a sharp mind for science, Henry's super talented and creative. Building props is a great fit for him. And no matter what Sam says, my wondering if I'll see him today is totally reasonable.

Someone emerges from a side stage door. From the human-gazelle movements, I easily identify the shadowy figure as Sam. She can't hide all her years of taking ballet. I cross over to meet her.

"Ready to go?" she asks after greeting me with a hug. "My mom's waiting outside."

"Already?" I say, a little disappointed. "I was hoping to watch one of your final rehearsals."

The scene on the stage has begun, so Sam whispers her answer. "No rehearsal for me today;

just costume fixes, which were super quick."

"Are you excited about the show?" I ask.

"I'm more nervous than excited," replies Sam.

"That's totally normal," I whisper back, giving her a reassuring pat on her arm. We've reached the exit doors, and I go back to speaking normally in the hallway. "You're gonna rock that stage, I just know it."

"Let's change the subject," Sam says. She really does seem nervous about this opening night. That's unusual, but I guess JFK Middle is a whole new ball game for her. It's the stage she's been dreaming about performing on for years. "Are you ready for your media training?"

Now it's my turn to release the belly butterflies. "I am. I just want to get to the point where I can walk up to a cafeteria table and introduce myself without looking awkward."

"That's a good goal to strive for," Sam teases.

"If I could work a room like Milo, I'd be pumped!" My voice echoes in the empty halls.

We round a corner and run straight into Henry.

"Hey! We were just talking about Milo and there you are," I say.

His eyes narrow in confusion. "What does Milo have to do with me?" he asks.

"Hey, Henry," Sam interrupts. "Archie just asked me if I'd seen you. He went to the prop room."

Archie is a crew member and Sam's not-so-secret crush.

"Uh, thanks," says Henry, avoiding eye contact with me. "See you guys."

Once we're out of earshot, Sam asks, "Did I miss something? Usually when he gets around you, Henry acts more puppy dog than *your* puppy dogs."

"Yeah, right," I say, knowing Sam is only teasing. She knows she's the one who's always going all heart-eyes emoji over one person or another. I've got too much on my plate to worry about boys. Even if it is a boy as cute—er, *cool*—as Henry.

"If you ask me, I think he's a little jealous," she says.

Stunned, I whisper at a higher octave than my speaking voice. "Jealous? Why would he be jealous? And of who?"

Sam shrugs a shoulder. "Just sayin'. Maybe you should lay off the Milo talk when he's around."

"I—*what*—?" With Sam's theory in mind, I

mentally go over my last interactions with Henry. *Ugh. I have been talking about Milo a lot.*

Sam happily drops the subject for the ride home in her mom's old yellow Beetle.

We barely buckle in before Sam's mom, Barbara, starts chatting with us. Her full head of blonde ringlets frame her excited face like sunflower petals. I love how she always seems to be cooking up fun ideas or working on quirky art projects. Sam isn't always on board at first—like when her mom decided their front lawn should be dotted with a flock of plastic flamingos—but she eventually comes around.

"Girls, I'm thinking of decorating the car with those happy/sad theater masks," Sam's mom is saying as we get out of the car. "I have an artist friend who can spray them on for me."

"Why would you do that?" Sam asks, sounding a bit mortified.

Her mom snakes an arm around Sam's shoulders and rests her cheek on top of Sam's head. "It's not every day my only child gets a speaking role in a big musical," she coos. "Am I right?"

Sam cracks a shy smile.

"You're right!" I confirm cheerily.

She lets go of Sam and tends to one of her crooked lawn flamingoes. "Don't worry," continues her mom. "It'll be tastefully done—like my friends here."

"Oh, well, in that case . . . ," Sam says, gesturing to her mom with perfect comedic timing.

Her mom bends and addresses the now perfectly upright flamingo. "You hear that? I knew she'd approve!"

My best friend and I are full-on giggling now. We shake our heads and enter Sam's house feeling lighter than when we left school.

The minute we step into her room, Sam guides

me to her full-length mirror and has me stand inches from it.

"Okay, let's work on speaking to your constituents," Sam begins. "Introduce yourself as if *she's* a voter." Sam nods toward my reflection.

I do as I'm told. Awkwardly.

"Good try," says Sam. "Now do it with a smile, and with more eye contact."

When I smile, my voice actually sounds friendlier.

Sam grins. "Okay. Again, but a little louder."

We try this exercise over and over, using Sam's different pointers each time—less fidgeting, more feeling—until, surprisingly, I start to improve.

"Okay, moving on," Sam says, handing me a microphone. She's clearly switched to director mode now. All she's missing is one of those chairs with her name on the back.

"Why do I need a mic?" I look at it like it's from the Planet Dadan, the wonky fictional world Galaxy Girl stumbles onto in issue 19. "I thought we were going to keep working on icebreakers."

"Did you forget about the Spirit Day town hall? You'll be onstage with the other candidates, and you'll have to talk into a microphone."

I make a face. "That's right."

"So here comes the Q. Just remember to speak into that mic like you own it," she says. "Stand straight, lift your chin, and give lots of eye contact all around the room."

Instead of sitting next to the pile of laundry on her bed and listening to my answer, she sets up her phone and points the camera at me from where she's standing.

I cringe. "Ugh, I have to do this on camera?"

"How else are you going to see what you need to work on?"

It's one thing to film my totally casual video diaries alone, and another to film me being interviewed. What kind of answers will people be expecting? What if I can't come up with the right words?

Sam's camera phone and serious face are pointed at me, and I wait for her to drill-sergeant scream, "Action!" but instead she plays a soft-spoken sixth grader and poses her question: "Now. Why should we vote for you, Hope?"

"Well, I, um, let's see—good question," I stammer, caught off guard and partly feeling silly because I'm not actually standing in front of a Spirit Day

crowd. I know I went over this question with Grace, but my mind is a complete blank. "Uh, I, hmmm. Let's see, I—"

Sam drops the soft-talker act and drill-sergeant shouts, "Cut!"

"Let me start over." I shake my head, hoping to clear out some of that nervousness.

"In a second," says Sam in the most nurturing voice. "Sorry about that. I was just trying to keep you from overthinking it. I can tell you're letting your nerves distract you."

I shake my head and sigh. "I'm ready to try again."

"Before we do another round, let's look at the video." Sam goes to her bed and pushes back a folded pile of shorts so we can sit.

It was super cringey seeing myself on camera. I keep making the most awkward faces, like someone is pinching me. And I can't seem to get a handle on who I want to be. First, I lean on one hip like I'm Miss Confident, and then I cross my arms like I want to disappear. And this happens all in the span of a few seconds. *Ugh.*

"You're used to filming vlogs," Sam points out. "But here you're not as natural and relaxed as you are on the videos you've shown me."

I sigh. *Am I hopeless?*

"Why does campaigning make me doubt myself so much?" I wonder aloud.

Sam puts her hand on mine. "Because the focus is more on *you* than your message. At least at first, as people get to know and trust you."

Sam explains that nailing the Q&A during the town hall can be as simple as turning up the dial on my normal personality, not trying to be someone else. I can't make up my strengths, only lean on them. This is exactly what Grace was saying about what Milo does.

Watching the video again and listening to Sam's feedback is helpful. But when I'm ready to film another trial run, my bestie has yet another surprise for me.

"I hope you don't mind," she says with a mischievous glint in her eye. "I invited a few friends over, and they just texted that they're here."

Lacy, Golda, and Charlie all plop down on Sam's bed and look at me. All they're missing is the popcorn.

"Let me tell you a little more about our test audience," Sam tells me. "Lacy here will represent the voters who are already on your side. She'll support you as long as you keep being the candidate she roots for."

Boy, I guess Sam is taking this media training more seriously than I thought. The girl is super prepared. I nod, ready to keep track of everyone's assigned roles.

"And Golda here is neutral—she's an undecided voter who isn't sold on any one candidate in particular."

Got it. I look at Golda, and she sighs, looks at her nails, and makes an unbothered face in the most overacting way. I almost crack up. But I know better not to laugh at any potential voter—especially one I need to win over.

"And finally we have Charlie, who represents a voter who is passionate about another candidate. She's got her mind made up, and it would surprise her if you were able to change it."

It isn't until Sam clears her throat at me that I think to break out with my new and improved introductions. I greet each "voter" individually and even remember to smile. After I'm done, Sam gives me a thumbs up.

They each have prepared questions for me, which I answer while keeping Sam's tips in mind. I can feel them pretending to judge me, for good or for bad. But keeping all the pointers in mind, my answers go way smoother this time. At the end of it all, we take a test vote and it's unanimous. I've won over Golda and Charlie. Lacy happily stays in my corner, too.

I turn to my coach, Sam. "What do you think?"

"Hmmm . . . still undecided," Sam says, then darts away laughing before I can catch her.

Charlie cues up some music, and Golda and Lacy start busting some slick dance moves. I crack up and pick up the mic and lip-sync the lyrics. Sensing it's safe for her to come back, Sam joins us, sharing my mic to chime in with the background vocals. Our work over, everyone is in play mode, and I'm so here for it.

Chapter 6

"**Y**ou're lucky I know a girl at the print shop," says my sister, Marie. She breezes into the kitchen and hands me the campaign shirts I asked for. "Otherwise, you would not have gotten these this fast."

"Wait, my hands are dirty!" A glob of ketchup is on my finger, so I try to catch the shirts with my forearm. They land on our pups, Cosmo and Rocket, instead. One of the tees blankets poor Rocket's eyes, and she shakes her head until it falls off her nose.

"Thank you so much, Marie!"

"Sure!" she shouts over her shoulder, already heading back to her bedroom. I detect a smile in her voice. She may never admit it, but it makes Marie happy to see me happy.

The moment my hands are clean, I inspect the shirts. They are gorgeous! Marie never does anything ordinary. This time, she's selected loose, flowy short-sleeved tees. In the center is a super-cute *"Gotta Have Hope"* logo, where the "v" in "have" looks like a check mark on a ballot.

I squeal at the top of my lungs and jump in place. These shirts are amazing, and I can't wait to rock them at school later.

I don't know if it's the T-shirts or the tips Sam gave me, but that day at school, I am ready to hit the campaign trail.

I'm eager to try out Sam's techniques, but I don't want to come off too strong, so I start with a subtle change. I give people in the sixth-grade locker area a little more eye contact than usual. If I happen to catch someone's eye, I respond with a friendly smile. And guess what? It makes a difference! People actually start to offer me a casual greeting here and there. It feels like a breakthrough.

Now is the time to level up. I pump myself up to actually speak.

"Hey," I call out to two kids heading in my direction.

"What's up?" one of them responds.

They want to know what's up, as in a campaign update? Oh no, I didn't think to prepare a statement.

My mouth goes dry. "Uh, I'm glad you asked." I channel Grace and parrot what she recently told me. "Our sixth-grade appreciation platform is polling well. Our constituents are really connecting to our message, and our volunteers are doing an amazing grassroots job canvassing and spreading the word about—"

"Dude, I don't need an oral report. I meant 'what's up' as in hello." The kids laugh and keep walking in the opposite direction.

Oh, duh. Way to turn off potential voters. But as awkward as this moment is, viewing it as a teachable moment helps me from getting *too* embarrassed.

And scoring a sweet treat as a consolation prize helps a bunch, too.

Camila brings a container of homemade campaign cookies to school. They're round sugar cookies topped with icing spelling out *Gotta Have Hope.*

"Ohmygosh, these look amazing," I tell Camila when I meet up with her and Grace at lunch. It strikes me yet again how talented and brilliant my friends all are. I'm super lucky to have them.

"Here's a list of people who've already been given cookies," says Grace. "These are the kids who really need to be shown appreciation. What do you think?"

I study the list and recognize the names of mathletes who just won a tournament. They never get as much attention as the athletes do. Also on the list are environmental club members and homework help volunteers.

"I think that's such a great idea, Grace," I say, clearing the choked-up emotion from my voice. "Thank you so much for doing that."

"Are you crying?" Camila teases.

"Some of us are just more in tune with our feelings." I pretend to be offended.

"Now it's your turn to hand deliver the rest to people," Grace continues. "And while you're at it, see if you pick up any talk about what people are looking for the next class president to accomplish. We'll use the answers as an unofficial poll."

"Sounds like a plan." I stand up and grab the

basket of cookies. "Go, team!" The three of us high-five each other, and then I set out on my own to walk the wilderness of our cafeteria.

Not all the kids at JFK Middle have lunch at the same time. Sam and Lacy eat later, for example. But I do recognize a few people, like Bella, who just rolled up to the table in the center of the cafeteria, where a few sixth and seventh graders are having an art club meeting. I start there first, leading with my eye contact, friendly smile, and loud, expressive voice.

"I love your shirt," Bella says after I give her and her friends cookies. "Is that one of your sister's designs?"

I nod. Being a fashionista herself, Bella is a huge Marie fan.

"It would be cool if Marie could come back to art club and share how high school is helping her designer goals."

"Bella, that is a great suggestion!" I say. "Students could come back and see the impact they've made and offer tips on what they've learned along the way."

I make a note of the idea, say goodbye, and move

on to another person I recognize. I'm happy to find Shep is not hanging with his friend Connor for once, so I head over to his table.

Ever since we had butted heads in science club, Connor's behavior toward me can be somewhat unpredictable. But for the most part, we stay out of each other's way, and I don't lose sleep over it.

Shep is grateful for the cookie, but he doesn't accept it without a wisecrack. "Will this hypnotize me into voting for you?" he asks as he downs his cookie in one bite.

"At the count of three, you will convince all your friends to vote Hope Roberts," I joke.

"Consider it done," he says in a monotone voice and bugged-out eyes. "Except for Connor. That would take a miracle."

"Well, we're all free to vote however we choose," I say. "The most important thing is we get to the polls."

I turn to leave and bump right into Connor.

"Were you guys talking about me?" he asks Shep as if I'm invisible. "I heard my name."

I ignore his rudeness and try to make nice. "Hope Roberts campaign cookie?" I offer him.

He finally makes eye contact with me. "Thanks,

but I'm voting for Mason. Good luck, though."

Good luck is usually a nice thing to wish some-one. But, *ouch*—Connor clearly meant it as an insult, like there's no way I can beat Mason. "Thank you," I say, hoping to douse the burn by keeping cool.

After I leave Shep's table, I think of the appreciation approach Grace has been taking. Instead of finding another table of familiar faces, I keep an eye out for the overlooked people. There, in the farthest corner of the cafeteria, is a quiet table with a group of sixth graders. They aren't speaking to each other, but reading, playing on their phones, or wearing headphones, zoned out. I go straight to them.

Even after practicing with Sam, it's still a little intimidating walking up to a table full of people you don't really know. It's a wonder how waiters do it! I take a deep breath and think about my message. I am helping sixth graders feel like an important part of the school. I want each of my classmates to feel seen and appreciated. I keep this in mind as I take the last few steps to the table.

"Uh, hi, how are you guys?" I begin. "I'm Hope Roberts, and I'm—"

"Running for sixth-grade class president," says Chloe, who's just walked over. She places her lunch tote and her journal on the table and takes a seat.

"Hey, Chloe," I say, happy to see a familiar face. "I'm just here to introduce myself and offer a sweet treat."

Everyone at the table is happy to take a cookie, except for Chloe.

"No thanks," she says with a kind smile.

I put away the cookie and smile back at her. I admire how she stays true to herself, despite what everyone around her is doing.

"Chloe is the only person on the planet who doesn't have a sweet tooth," says the girl sitting at the end of the table.

Chloe raises an eyebrow and smirks to herself. "I

guess that means I'll be the only person in seventh period who's not struggling to stay awake."

"So that's the secret to avoiding that two o'clock crash." Her friend shakes her head. "Bring your own lunch every day."

"When they start offering less sugary choices here, maybe I'll take a break from always packing lunch," says Chloe.

"Oooh." Her friend sits up taller. "Or when they start serving breakfast all day, I'll be the first in line."

Chloe nods, smirking. "But first this school has to take care of more pressing issues," says Chloe. "Like investigating whether the tiger statue really does come alive at night."

Someone at the table startles us with a lifelike

"Rawr!" and we all gasp and crack up.

"This table has more ideas than I can keep up with!" I grin. "You know, I'd like to think about how I can help get different lunch options on the cafeteria menu."

Chloe gives me a nod, and it feels great seeing a sign that she approves. The girl knows her stuff—about flyer designs, eating healthy, and obviously super-cute journals. I care about her opinions and want to hear more of them.

"Here's wishing you all a bright-eyed seventh period," I tease as I walk away.

It's amazing how not shying away from voters makes me feel more confident about campaigning—and kind of excited. Who knew that the only way to get here was by doing the thing I was afraid of?

I actually may have a shot at winning this thing!

Chapter 7

Grace is right again. (That's why she's the best campaign manager.) Listening to voters' needs is an important part of campaigning. If you have no idea what voters' concerns are, how can you represent them in office? Without the listening skills the job requires, how can you even speak on behalf of an entire group of people?

With my boost in confidence, I'm hoping the more I show everyone that I'm a willing listener, the more people will talk openly with me about the ways they want our school to change. I start keeping a list of their concerns to go over with Grace at our next meeting.

It's study period for a lot of sixth graders, so I am continuing my boots-on-the-ground work.

"Hi, I'm Hope Roberts, and I'm running for sixth-grade class president," I say to the girl who's just walked out of the school library. She reminds me of Marie because she looks like she could possibly be the coolest person in the school.

She stops and wordlessly reads the campaign flyer I hand her before looking squarely at me.

"Hi, Hope Roberts, I'm Naomi Francois, and *I'm* running for sixth-grade class president."

Oh.

"H-hi, Naomi. Nice to finally meet you," I say. "Congrats!" I hold out my hand for a high five rather than a handshake for some reason. Naomi *so* doesn't look like the high five type. She looks at my palm for a few seconds before giving it a weak tap with her fingers. "I'll take a flyer if you have one," I offer.

"No," she says, not clearing up if she meant no, she doesn't have one, or no, she doesn't want to give me one. I would believe it if she didn't have one. I haven't seen any of her posters or leaflets around the school. "But good luck to you," she says before walking away.

I spot Chloe about to enter the library, and she walks over to say hi. "Hello again."

"Hiya," I say, cheering up. "Heading over to study?"

"I'm just going to write in my journal and chill. How about you?"

LIBRARY

"Handing out flyers, meeting the constituents," I say.

Chloe points her head toward a chatty group of kids wearing team tracksuits heading this way. "Now's your chance," she whispers.

"Hi, guys," I call out to them. "Hope Roberts for

sixth-grade class president." No one comes to grab the flyers I'm holding out. "Maybe they didn't hear me," I tell Chloe. She shrugs.

I almost talk myself out of trying again, but then I recognize one of their faces.

"Hey, Miss MVP?" I call out to the tall girl I witnessed Milo joking around with the other day. That nickname gets their attention. But it remains to be seen if that's a good thing or a bad thing.

The tall girl steps out from the group. "What did you call me?"

I gulp. That exchange with Naomi doesn't seem so scary now. "Uh, that's what Milo calls you. Right?"

No response. Instead, everyone is looking at me like I'm barking instead of talking. *We definitely didn't cover this during media training.*

"Because of your epic game the other day," I add. Finally, the tall girl smiles the sweetest dimpled smile. I start kicking my imaginary soccer ball. "The way you handled that ball was awesome."

I don't stop to wonder why it is I'm making things up. I didn't go to her game! Maybe it's something you do when you're in survival mode.

"What are you doing?" Her teammate with a ponytail laughs, pointing to the herky-jerky movements of my feet. "You don't kick a volleyball."

"Oh, that's just her happy dance," says quick-thinking Chloe.

Miss MVP looks genuinely touched to hear it. "Aw, finally a JV team fan. Want to come to our scrimmage? We're heading over to the gym now."

I was hoping to meet as many people as possible this period, and I won't be able to do that if I spend it all with one group of people. "Well, I'm actually in the middle of—"

Chloe places a gentle hand on my arm. I trust her instincts enough to drop the point I'm making. "That's so cool of you guys," Chloe says. "She can come for a few minutes, right, Hope?"

I shake my head and come to my senses. JV teams are mostly made up of sixth graders, and by the sounds of it, they don't often get the shine that older players do. So this outing will be all part of showing sixth graders they're appreciated.

Chloe and I follow behind the team and only chat when we're out of earshot.

"It'll be fun," starts Chloe. "Hang out a few minutes, shake hands, and get a photo. Ask them if it's okay if you put their photo on a campaign poster. Everyone loves to see themselves represented, so they'll probably agree. It'll help promote the team *and* your campaign. I'll come with you and take the pics."

"Thank you," I say, grateful. "Are you sure I'm not taking time from your writing plans?"

"Are you kidding me? This will be way more inspiring than sitting by myself. I'll have that much more to write about."

We have such a great time at the gym. At one point, Miss MVP, whose name we learn is Emma, asks me to get in on the game. I boldly accept the ball and mimic what I'd watched Emma do moments before.

But before I do, I shout, "Hope Roberts, here to serve!"

The ball careens right into a torn corner of the net. I can almost hear tires screeching as all the action comes to a halt. The closest girl to the net can't seem to untangle the ball, so players from both sides try and help.

"Did my power serve just burn a hole through that net?" I joke a little too soon.

No one laughs, and I don't blame them. It's not right that the JV team has to play with janky equipment like this.

"I'll add new volleyball equipment to my list," I mutter to Chloe, pulling out my phone.

"Oh, wow, you can get us a new net?" Emma asks. "That's so awesome of you!"

Chloe flashes me a worried look and I make an SOS face at her.

"Um, n-n-no," I stammer.

Before I know it, the entire team drowns me out with thank-yous and pats on the back. And they don't give me a chance to correct them before the bell rings.

But this is what sixth-grade appreciation is all about . . . right?

Chapter 8

When your ears are open and you really pay attention, it's amazing what you can pick up. Beyond my direct chats with potential voters, I keep my ears open around school and start noticing conversations in restrooms, hushed discussions in the library, and mouthfuls of chatter in the cafeteria.

"I can barely fit my presentation into my locker. Do they expect me to carry it all day when my presentation is last period?"

Interesting. I pause to take notes on my phone. A solution for this could be a holding area for bigger items. Or maybe even bigger lockers. Sixth-grade lockers are much smaller than the rest of the school's. And it's not like we have way less home-work or textbooks to carry. Something's gotta change.

As I step out the girls' bathroom, I overhear a boy complain to his teacher. "This is the second field trip my older brother's been on, and our grade hasn't gone anywhere yet."

"Focus on Friday's test and then we'll talk," says the teacher before slipping back into her classroom.

More field trips, I document in my phone. Except I don't realize I've also said that out loud. The boy gives me and my note taking the side eye.

"You a reporter for the school paper or some-thing?" he asks.

"Uh, no," I say. "I'm making a list of things sixth graders would like to see happen at JFK. I hope to help get their needs met."

"Cool," he answers, suddenly holding his head up the way Cosmo does after he's been to the groomers. Could it be the boost from knowing someone cares about his concerns? "How long is your list so far?" he asks.

"It's growing."

"Nice." He nods. "Well, I'll keep my fingers crossed for all of us."

It feels good knowing you improved someone's mood, at least a little. But it isn't until the boy and I part ways that I realize I forgot to tell him about my campaign. *Ugh!* Talking about myself to strangers is getting easier, but it still feels weird to tell people I'll do something for them in exchange for their vote. The fact is, I want people to know I really care about sixth graders. For me, it's not just about winning the election.

I'll work on my introductions as I work on this wish list.

There's got to be a way I can take a small but important wish on the list and make it happen—to prove to the sixth-grade class that I really do want to help. *But which one?*

I know Grace can help me decide.

Great work talking to the voters, texts Grace in reply to the list I've sent her. I don't point out to her that some info on that list was actually overheard.

"Heads up, Hope!" I look up from my cell phone just in time to sidestep Chloe, but she sidesteps at the same time. We smack right into each other, knocking her journal to the floor.

"Are you texting anything about the texting-and-walking rule at JFK Middle?" she jokes. "Lucky I don't work for the paper, or there could be a candidate scandal going on there."

I chuckle and pick up her journal. "Totally my bad. Thanks for not reporting me to the press."

"I wouldn't do that," she answers. "You're one of the good guys. You opened up the locker area entrance for a day. Legend."

Hearing that makes me smile. "Here's your journal," I say. "I'm sure you want to keep it safe."

"I just like to take notes before I forget about stuff," she says with a grin. "It's more like an ideas journal than a diary."

"Ideas about what?" I ask, hoping my scientific curiosities are not coming across as nosy.

"Anything from lunch ideas and my personal reading list to the new vocabulary words I pick up."

I nod, thinking of Galaxy Girl's activity log and how it helps her stay on mission. "And do you cross off the ideas once you accomplish them?"

"It's not really a to-do list," says Chloe. "Some of the ideas never go anywhere, but that's okay with me. I know they'll inspire me to get things done in other ways."

"Cool," I say. Even though I probably would use an idea journal as more of a list of goals to accomplish, I appreciate Chloe's way of doing things. She's super thoughtful, which is awesome.

People scatter in different ways, and the walk to my next class is enough to air out my thoughts. Chloe sounds like the perfect resource for sixth-grade feelings on different topics.

I wonder if she'd be interested in joining my campaign . . .

"Hi, Ms. Reimer," I greet the vice principal as she's about to step into her office.

"How can I help you, Miss Roberts?" she asks politely, though her words sound clipped.

"I just wanted to thank you again for opening the sixth-grade entrance. It was a hit."

"So I've heard," she says, looking at me from the corner of her eyes. "Congrats to you for providing such a special privilege to your fellow classmates."

"Thank you, Ms. Reimer," I say.

"But that can't be the only reason you're here."

Ms. Reimer is onto me.

"I was wondering . . . ," I start. Ms. Reimer shows me her back and enters her office. I hesitate for a moment, wondering if I'm supposed to follow her.

"Can't hear you from there, Roberts," she shouts from her office.

When I enter the room, she's already seated at her desk, poring through the pages of a binder.

"A few of the sixth graders were wondering why our grade doesn't have any plans for a field trip yet."

Ms. Reimer peers over her glasses for a second. My grimaced face freezes, and I brace myself for her

response. "That can't be right."

"I—I checked different calendars and there's no field trip listed. In comparison, the seventh graders have already gone on two trips this year."

"Well, that just won't do. We must have overlooked something. I have a faculty meeting in the morning, so I'll find out what is amiss and get back to you."

Get back to me? Is this really happening? I totally didn't expect this adult to talk to me like she owes me something. But in this case, it's true. We are owed an explanation and a resolution. I sit up taller to reflect that fact, and to my surprise, Ms. Reimer shakes my hand on my way out.

Knowing Ms. Reimer is looking into the field trip

situation makes me so glad I spoke up. I don't want to slow this progress down.

♡ ☑ ☆

The next week, I do more listening to what kids are buzzing about. The more I hear, the more tapped in I feel to what students are looking for.

I'm eager to help! And a lot of kids seem eager to *get* my help, like they trust that I can make things happen. With the shortcut entrance success, many of them realize I've worked to change something before, and I can do it again. I'm so touched by their confidence in me; I'm pumped to do more.

The next morning, I run into Ms. Reimer in the school's entrance, right next to the ginormous JFK

tiger mascot statue.

"Miss Roberts, I want you to be the first to know," says Ms. Reimer, her block heels clacking in the echoey space. "The sixth-grade field trip has been reinstated."

I almost squeal right there in front of her. And just when she was starting to respect me more. "It has?" I ask, sounding way more surprised than I intended to.

"There was a misunderstanding between our school and the camp facility's manager. Luckily, they still reserved our annual slot."

"Camp facility?" I ask, a little nervous that I just snared the entire sixth grade into an uncool situation. I picture us all roughing it and sleeping with one eye open in some alligator-infested swamp. After all, this is Florida.

"Yes, the Grove Nature Preserve. It really is a wonderful place. It will be a two-day study of our glorious ecosystem and what we need to do to protect it."

"Wow, that sounds amazing," I say, excited. "Thank you!"

"No, thank you, Hope, for bringing this matter to

our attention. It should not have dragged on for that long, but I'm glad we were able to save the sixth-grade field trip."

"Me too," I say, beaming. I want to tell everyone this news, right away. Like, shout it out from Earth's exosphere. But I linger.

Ms. Reimer raises an eyebrow. "What is it?"

"Nothing major, really," I begin, trying my chances while I have Ms. Reimer's attention. "It's just that—well, do you think we can have more recycling bins on each floor?"

Ms. Reimer's nasally voice rings through the atrium. "Last I checked, we had plenty."

I start talking with my words and my hands. "There are bins on each floor, yes, but only on one side.

It would help to have bins on both ends of the halls."

"Noted," she answered, nodding thoughtfully, pausing before saying, "I'll look into it."

"Thank you, Ms. Reimer," I say as she starts down the hall. "Thank you."

I speed-walk straight to the sixth-grade lockers and find the boy who complained about our lack of field trips.

"We've got our sixth-grade field trip back!" I announce to him, loud enough for others to hear and huddle around. "We're heading on an overnight trip at a very cool nature preserve."

The boy gets a daydreamy look on his face before nodding at me. "Nature is good."

"I was hoping more for Disney," one voice calls

out. "But that's better than nothing."

"Hey, could you get us a Disney trip, too?" says someone else.

"Before we make it to Disney, we should get to tour NASA first. It's a lot closer," says a girl standing to my right.

Instead of a pat on the back, I just get more demands. My thumbs are flying over my phone, but I can barely keep up with all the wishes being tossed at me at a breakneck rate. It's overwhelming.

To keep from running away from all this pressure, I focus on the good feeling I have from delivering on that field trip. Doing this makes me realize something: These kids believe in JFK Middle again. They feel hopeful about the cool things that could happen here. If granting one wish from my list could do this, then I'd like to try granting more.

But the twist in my stomach reminds me how scary it could be to go down this road. Not just because of overwhelming moments like now, but because of the potential for things to go wrong.

And I can't let everyone down.

Chapter 9

Lunchtime is the perfect chance to bring up my new campaign focus with Grace. I get Grace's whole idea of coming up with one message and sticking to it like a proton would a neutron. But I'm on a wish-granting roll! First the sixth-grade locker entrance win, and now the field trip. Sure, it's scary knowing I may end up disappointing some people. But granting just a few wishes is better than none. Why stop now?

"The campaign is about boosting sixth-grade appreciation, and being a good listener so they know their concerns matter," Grace reminds me between crunchy bites of her hard-shell taco. "Not being some magician granting wishes to everyone."

Somehow over the past few days, our lunch table at the cafeteria has become campaign headquarters.

"Um, I think you got your magicians mixed up with your fairy godmothers," I tease, unable to resist.

Camila leans back in her seat and grins. "She's got a point there."

Grace gives me a smirk. "Um, I think you got campaigning mixed up with community service."

"What's the difference?" I ask, genuinely curious.

Grace looks stumped for a second. Her eyes dart to Camila's before she answers. "Okay, so maybe they are related," says Grace. "But we can't veer off course now. You only have a few weeks to rack up votes and get the word out about your campaign."

"But it's not just about votes, it's about making a difference," I say. "You should've seen this kid's face when I told him about the field trip. He seemed inspired to help make a difference, too."

Camila looks touched. "What do you have to top that?" she asks Grace.

Grace faces her tablet screen toward us. "After talking to a test group of voters, it looks like you are polling ahead of Naomi Francois, and slightly behind Mason Taylor."

"That's great!" I squeal. It's way better than I expected. Naomi and Mason went to a larger elementary school with the majority of kids in the sixth grade, so I came into this election as a lesser-known candidate.

"But that's on your sixth-grade appreciation platform. Switching up your approach this close to Spirit Day could confuse people who are starting to get a handle on who you are. Your poll numbers could go down."

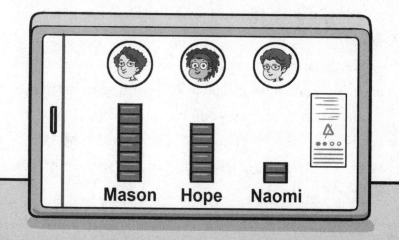

"We don't know that for sure," I say with a hopeful tone in my voice. "What if it just helps them get to know me better?"

"I think there's room for both of you to be right," interrupts Camila.

"Agreed," I say, raising my juice box as if making a toast. "Why can't I push for sixth graders' appreciation *and* get a new net for our JV volleyball team at the same time?"

"Because there are limits to the class president's budget and power. The office is about being a leader and representing sixth graders at student council meetings," explains Grace. "Didn't you read the student government handbook I gave you?"

I immediately feel guilty. I haven't had time with all the campaigning and wish list building I've been doing.

"Suggestions are helpful because they can lead to change," continues Grace in full campaign manager mode. "And sure, you need to know what their concerns are. But it's impossible to grant all their wishes. Promising them anything will only get yourself in trouble."

"Fine, I'll think things over," I say. I can't shake

the thought that sixth graders would be happy if progress was made. I don't get why I can't get ahead in the polls *and* give the kids what they're hoping for. I can't just give up on them.

A lightbulb switches on in my head. I think I just found my next campaign slogan. But I don't share this with the table. I think they'd only talk me out of it, and this idea deserves a try.

"All I'm asking is that you please let me know before you make any more decisions like this," Grace says, reaching for her pinging phone. "I want to be able to manage any hiccups while they're still small."

All of a sudden, Grace sucks in air like she's just heard something shocking.

"That was more of a gasp than a hiccup," says Camila, eager to ease the tension at the table.

"What is it?" I ask.

Grace puts down her water bottle and turns to me. "There are now only two candidates remaining for sixth-grade class president. Naomi Francois just dropped out."

My jaw hangs. That is totally unexpected news.

"Oh my goodness, is she okay?" I ask.

Grace nods. "Maybe she just got cold feet or something."

I don't blame her. We *are* getting close to Spirit Day. I try not to think that far ahead. For now, this news has lit an urgency in me that I can't ignore.

Before lunch is over, I race back to my locker. I keep a stash of campaign materials in there, in case I need them. A few mini posters and a big black Sharpie should do the trick.

I know this is going against Grace's advice, but I just can't give up on my classmates. They deserve to have someone try their hardest to help them feel

heard. Besides, isn't that what sixth-grade appreciation is about—reminding them they should hold on
to hope that things will change?

I scribble what comes to mind on each poster.

HOPE for Better Cafeteria Food.

HOPE for Field Trips.

HOPE for Change.

After I post a *HOPE for Change* poster near my
locker, I go to one of the most crowded areas of the
school building—the front entry.

The snarling tiger frozen in attack mode will
hopefully watch over my poster and scare away any

prankster kid intent on pulling it down. Milo's slick-looking campaign poster is already on one side of the wall, undisturbed. I go to the opposite wall and find the perfect spot near Mason Taylor's straightforward acronym poster.

MASON = Motivate. Advocate. Support. Outreach. Next 6th Grade Class President!

I pause, wondering which places to hit next. I only started sixth grade a couple months ago, so I'm not totally familiar with the different parts of the school building.

There's always the area outside the cafeteria. But, no, Grace and Camila will just be finishing up their lunch, and I'll bump into them there. Maybe the library entry hall?

I head there and hang up a poster right outside the double door entrance.

"Hope for field trips," I hear someone read aloud. Chloe's just strolling out of the library. "It has a nice ring to it."

"You think?" I smile.

"Sure," she says, examining the poster carefully. "And fancy lettering."

"Thanks!"

Chloe eyes the small stack pinned under my arm. "Let's see what else you've got."

I hold the posters up to Chloe and cycle through them like someone in a classic movie scene. She reads them silently, her eyes thoughtfully scanning each one.

"What do you think?" I ask with wiggling *ta-da!* fingers.

"Nice!" she says, giving me the thumbs-up. "Where to next?"

I pause and make a face. "Not sure. I want to put these in more crowded areas, but I can't think of too many of them."

Chloe raises an arm and points. "The makers' space on the other end of this floor is right outside a few popular sixth-grade classrooms."

There's a sixth-grade hangout I don't know about? I realize for the first time that because of my advanced classes, I spend most of my time in a way different area than most sixth graders.

"Thank you, Chloe," I say. "I appreciate you helping me spread some inspiration."

"Inspiration?" she asks playfully as she walks away. "Oh, so in this case, your posters are more like my journal ideas and not your to-do lists."

As I head in the opposite direction, toward the makers' space, Chloe's last words echo under my big curls. *Don't people* need *to be inspired before they can help bring about change?*

Above everything else, I want these messages to motivate people to dream big. I hope that's the impression my posters make on people.

How could they read it any other way?

Chapter 10

"**H**ow mad is she?" I ask Camila on our way to science club. This will be the first time I've seen Grace since I hung up my new posters.

She shakes her head. "Grace isn't really the mad type. She's more . . . concerned."

If I know Grace, that means she's recalculating the numbers on all those spreadsheets she loves making. She'll probably decide to conduct a new poll to find out just how much the posters hurt or helped our campaign.

I scan the science lab when we walk in. Grace isn't here yet. And I know Henry won't be able to make it today because tonight is opening night for the musical.

Camila and I take our seats at the table to the left. Soon after, Connor walks in wearing his trademark smirk. Shep is at his side, grinning at whatever Connor's just said. It's a shame how normal Shep acts when he's not around his smug friend. I expect Connor to just walk by without more than his usual side eye, but he actually comes right up to me.

"Hey, I can't remember if I gave you one of these," says Connor, handing me a VOTE FOR MASON button.

Not able to hold in his snicker any longer, Connor laughs at his own prank. But the joke's on him. I get to check out Mason Taylor's campaign swag up close. It's actually pretty cute. Definitely better than his acronym posters. And it's a good reminder that I need to pay closer attention to my election opponent.

Grace shuffles in at the same time as our advisor/science teacher, Mr. Gillespie. When I wave to her, Grace nods back. She doesn't smile, but the nod is a reassuring sign. "Can you believe the musical is opening tonight?" Camila asks me, probably sensing the whiff of tension between me and Grace.

I smile from ear to ear. "This has been Sam's dream for so long. I'm super excited for her."

"Thanks for going to see it with us tomorrow, even though you're already going tonight," whispers Camila.

"No prob—"

"Settle down," says Mr. Gillespie.

He sounds like he did earlier today in class, when he'd asked us to get ready for a pop quiz.

Mr. Gillespie sets us up for our newest group science project, and then steps out of our way to let us collaborate the best way we see fit.

The more time we all spend together, the less tense things are between me and Grace. She's in a relaxed mood as the three of us walk out of the lab together an hour later.

"So, Grace, what'd you think of my new posters?" I finally ask in a little voice.

Grace frowns and then shrugs. "The penmanship is eye-catching. But the posters were a risk I wouldn't have advised taking." She touches a finger to her chin. "Oh wait, now I remember that I actually *did* advise against it."

"Okay, maybe she *is* a little mad," says Camila, holding up her fingers like she's pinching the air.

"Some risks are worth taking," I gently remind Grace. "And I think this was one of them."

"Well, I'll keep an ear out to see how it will affect your polls."

"Thanks, Grace," I say. "And I'm sorry I went behind your back. That wasn't fair to you and all the work you're doing to help."

Grace sighs and lets the corner of her lips stretch into an understanding smile.

Camila puts her arms around the both of us, relieved that we talked this out.

"Hey," I ask them both. "Did you guys know there's a makers' space and it's a sixth-grade hangout spot?"

Camila shakes her head no at the same time Grace nods yes.

"Where do you guys think I conducted my poll?" Grace asks.

I turn to Camila. "We need to venture out of our advanced-class bubble more often."

Camila's laughter sounds muffled through her facepalm.

♡ ☑ ☆

I've been to a few of Sam's performances before, but this one feels extra special.

"This place looks just like I remember it," says Marie, who is sitting next to me a few rows back from the stage.

Two rows ahead of us is Sam's mom. She was never one to worry about sitting too close. For me, it's tough to suspend all belief when you're able to see the flurry of real-world activity going on in the wings. She must feel me staring at the back of her head, because she turns and gives me an excited wave. I return it as enthusiastically and chuckle.

When the lights dim and the orchestra fills the space with the sounds of strings layered over thumping percussion, I do a happy dance in my seat and the packed audience applauds in anticipation. When the heavy velvet curtains open, my jaw drops. The set design is gorgeous. Henry, Archie, and the rest of the stage crew did an amazing job. When the actors begin unraveling the story, I'm hooked right away.

It's not long before Sam and Lacy make their appearances. They fall into their roles like naturals. Right before my eyes, Sam goes through this transformation where she's no longer Sam, but another girl entirely. And it's so much fun getting to know this new person. Both Sam and Lacy get great reactions from the crowd, who laugh, gasp, and sigh at all the right moments.

By the time the show is over, I'm beaming with pride and cheering at the top of my lungs as the entire cast take their bows. The wolf whistles and standing ovation is their final confirmation that they killed it!

After a few minutes of waiting near the backstage door, we all cheer "Congratulations!" when our stage stars walk out. I hand Sam a bouquet of colorful flowers after she hugs her mom. Her arms already look overloaded with arrangements.

"You were amazing!" I tell her.

Sam is giddy and breathless. "I can't believe I get to do this all weekend!"

Lacy rushes over and wraps us in a group hug. "Did you all enjoy the show?" she asks with a bright smile.

"We loved it!" we say without hesitation.

People walking by recognize my friends and congratulate them, and then two special well-wishers stop by—Archie and Henry.

"Awesome performance, you two," Archie says.

Sam goes all googly-eyed and can't stop smiling. When Henry looks at me and waves hello, I'm hopeful things between us aren't weird anymore.

But then a voice I don't recognize shouts my name. I assume there's another Hope around until he calls out a second time. "Hey, Hope Roberts!"

Oh, he does *mean me.*

A sixth-grade boy in costume walks over. He was an ensemble cast member in the show. A few students recognize my name and walk over to meet me, too. This has never happened before, so it must have something to do with my campaign's new wish list focus. I'm not sure how to act, and for a panicked second, I think of giving them all an elaborate handshake, like Milo would.

"Could you really get us better cafeteria food?" asks a tall girl to my right.

"Is it true you plan to grant all of the sixth graders' requests?" says a voice coming from behind me. Startled, I look back, realizing there are a few more kids there, standing close.

I would gulp if I could, but my throat goes crackly dry again. Everyone's eyes look so eager—almost like Cosmo's and Rocket's when they're watching me eat.

"Well, Hope?" the tall girl pushes for my answer.

"Hope—" someone else nudges.

My stomach twists. "Actually, I n-never—" I stammer, but stop speaking altogether when I catch a glimpse of Sam's face behind the crowd. She's been completely edged out on her special night.

I can't do this to my best friend. And this is so not what I'm here for. That reality check instantly smooths the knots in my stomach and helps me find my voice.

"I'll answer all of your questions at next Friday's

town hall," I explain to everyone as I reach a hand through the crowd for Sam. She uses it as a lifeline to get to my side, and we link arms. "Tonight, I'm just a proud bestie and a fan of this amazing show. I hope you tell your friends and come back to see it again!"

Crisis averted, the crowd respects my request and disperses, leaving us to enjoy a friend group selfie to commemorate opening night.

It feels good to take a break from all the campaigning for one night. But I can't wait until I get back to it on Monday.

Chapter 11

The musical had the best opening weekend. I went to see the show a second time with Camila, Grace, Golda, and Charlie, and it was even better than opening night. Grace and I only spoke about campaign plans once, and that was to quickly go over our game plan for the days leading up to Friday's Spirit Day.

JFK Middle's Spirit Day is legendary in the Space Coast area. According to tradition, we don't just pump up our winning athletics program, but all the academic and social ones, too! All week, everyone rocks school colors: maroon and yellow. The tiger statue even wears a JFK Tigers scarf and hat. The forecast for Friday's weather is sunny and clear—because, Florida. This means all the events will take place on our home field—including the town hall.

We've been assigned our very own Vote for Hope Spirit Day booth. On Friday, we plan to wear our campaign shirts and hand out more treats, stickers, and buttons. We'll also have a suggestion box to manage all the wishes that may pour in (Grace's brilliant idea). But we're still debating what gimmicky fun will attract more booth visitors. Grace thinks a dartboard would be popular, but I'm not so sure.

One thing's for certain: I need to explore the campus more before then. There must be more student hangout spots I've never visited. What if someone asks me a question about campus I can't answer?

Monday before the morning bell, I venture from my usual comfort zone to the far end of the building, where art covers the walls. I follow the muffled sounds of drumbeats and horns blaring until I find the room where band practice is just coming to an end.

The double doors swing open and a stream of

students carrying instruments trickle out. A lot of them look like sixth graders. I bob and weave as I try to cross their path. Suddenly, someone trumpets the first few notes of the national anthem, and another person follows that up with the cymbals. The sound is so piercing, up close, and unexpected that I freeze in my tracks. Practically my whole body shudders with the final cymbal clash.

"That was for you, oh presidential candidate!" A girl carrying a shiny brass instrument steps right in front of me.

"Oh, th-thank you." I give her a grateful smile.

"Hey, do you need a theme song for your campaign? Because we got you," she adds, holding up her instrument.

"Let's play her that song you made up this morning!" the drummer says while tapping a steady beat.

I spy an irate teacher storming toward us with her arms waving wildly. "Aw, that's okay," I say. "But it's cool of you to offer."

"She doesn't want to hear us," pouts the boy with the cymbals. "She just wants our votes."

My upper lip begins to sweat the way it does sometimes when I'm overwhelmed. "No, it's not that.

I just don't want you to get into trouble for playing in the—"

"We'll vote for you if you can get the school to have a spring jazz concert," the girl with the trumpet says, her eyes flashing her excitement.

"You should vote for whoever feels right," I respond. "But I can't promise—"

Luckily, the angry band teacher saves me from having to finish. I take her entrance as my cue to escape. Just beyond the hall, I spot an exit door leading to a leafy courtyard.

Outside, I take a deep, calming breath and check out the courtyard scene. There's an empty bench between two palm trees that makes the perfect setup for a little scientific observation.

The rest of the space is filled mostly with older kids swallowing down their breakfasts or doing last-minute homework. A few others toss a football back and forth or are just meeting up to chat and chill. I take notes on my phone.

After a few minutes, I come up with a hypothesis— the courtyard isn't the first choice for a majority of sixth graders. This is probably because the courtyard is popular with older kids, who can be

intimidating. I'm just about to pack up and leave when there's a sudden change in the flow of courtyard activity. Milo is walking through, and his presence has caused a few to break from their pattern.

From this close up, I can see how Milo works his magic. I have a few burning questions I'd love to see answered. Namely, are people always asking *him* for stuff, too? What does he promise them? And how does he handle letting them down?

But I don't want to bombard Milo with questions this early, like the band kids did to me. Instead, I duck out of sight behind the tall shrub by the trash can. That way I'm within earshot, and I can record and analyze the data without being detected.

"Hey, that was a great drum solo," Milo tells a lanky boy in a vintage concert tee.

"How did your presentation go?" Milo asks a boy wearing a hoodie.

When a girl in an arm cast skateboards by, Milo pulls out the perfect marker. "I remembered to bring it this time!" he says before signing a spot on her cast.

So far, I'm not hearing him mention anything close to campaign promises. Maybe I need to get closer. I hunch over a bit too far and get a whiff of what's molding in the trash.

"Hope? You okay?" I spring upright to see Henry at my side.

Busted. *He must really think I'm obsessed with Milo now.*

That's when my nerves kick in and I start speed-talking like my tongue is on fire. "Hi, Henry, how are you? Your set design was so amazing—I'm not sure I had a chance to tell you that. I was just checking out this courtyard; it's my first time hanging out here, so . . ."

The early bell could not have gone off at a more ideal time. Henry's confused expression is unchanged as I wave goodbye and zip across the courtyard back to my corner of the world.

As my surroundings get more familiar, so do the students. A few of them catch up to me in the halls. But most of the sixth graders who approach me seem to have latched onto my new message as campaign promises. They want to know more about what I plan to do to fulfill what's on the posters.

"Do we get to decide what the new cafeteria food will be?" one girl asks.

"Yeah, and where we'll go on the field trips?" another guy adds.

Oh no.

"That's not what the posters mean," I try to explain again. They're walking with me now. "They are meant to inspire us into believing we can work *together* to make things happen."

If I can only make it to my class at the end of the hall, I can hide away from everything in there.

"But we *are* getting a field trip, thanks to you," the girl is saying to me now.

"Yes, but—"

"So that means you *have* been working on things," squeals another boy, catching up to her to the right.

Before I know it, someone in the hall shouts, "Hope is making things happen!" and a few people whoop and cheer.

"Did she really change the cafeteria food already?" a guy with a booming voice shouts out. "Can't wait for lunch period!"

"N-no, no," I tell them.

"Do they have gluten-free pizza?" someone asks the booming voice guy.

"Ooo, I'm getting the gluten-free pizza!" the girl next to me yells.

My heart starts beating faster, but before I can speak up and handle the situation, the second bell clears the hallways in a flash. I don't get the chance to explain that the messages on my posters aren't promises.

By the time I make it to Spanish class, I'm winded and overwhelmed. All I wanted to do was listen to people's hopes.

How did I get here?

Chapter 12

Later that day at our lunch table slash campaign headquarters, I'm getting way too many disappointed stares from kids carrying trays with regular, gluten-filled pizza. I even hear a boy scoff to a friend, "There goes *false Hope*."

I have to steel myself and ignore my strong urge to flee the scene and hide out in the science lab pantry, where there are other specimens just as tired of being dissected. Needless to say, I'm now operating in crisis mode.

After downloading to Grace and Camila everything that happened that morning, Grace makes a face like she's just had too much to eat.

"The first thing we need to do is take down those posters," she says. "Like, now."

"Already done," I say, opening my bag to reveal the rolled-up posters I rushed around snatching off the walls right before lunch.

Grace nods her approval. "That's a good call if we are going to put a stop to all these unrealistic expectations."

Expectations that I've somehow encouraged.

I appreciate Grace not using this time to say she told me so. If she did want to do that, no one would fault her. Though—*ouch*, it would sting pretty bad.

"I don't get it," says an exasperated Camila. "Hope's actions and track record prove she's no phony. Why can't they see that?"

"They're so focused on their disappointment," I mutter.

Camila gives my shoulder a comforting rub.

"We just have to get back on message and reveal more of the real Hope," suggests Grace.

I think about how little most voters know about
the real me. I've been too busy flashing staged
smiles or practicing how to be an all-seeing, all-
hearing fly on the wall. If I had the chance to tell
them one or two things about myself, what would I
show them?

Grace fires up her tablet and starts tapping the
screen. "According to my questionnaires, what
people like most about Hope is that she's smart,
takes risks, and seems to really care about voters."

"Wow," I say, touched. "That's so sweet."

Grace taps her screen a few more times. "And I've
been keeping an ear out for Mason Taylor's Spirit
Day plans. Word is, he'll be showing off his drawing
skills and creating free caricatures for every person
who visits his booth."

Camila gasps. "Now that's really cool!"

I nod and stop myself from figuring out how I can manage a quick visit to Mason's booth. "I know I'm the one who led us down this road, but may I make a suggestion?" I ask.

"Of course," says Grace.

"Well, if we want people to know the real me, I'd love to somehow bring in my love for science. Like, at our Spirit Day booth, instead of going with the dartboard as our gimmicky fun, maybe I can work a science trick."

"That's one way to put some personality into the campaign," says Camila. "But couldn't that be kind of complicated?"

"Science has never let me down," I say to both of them. Grace's finger is tapping her chin in thought, and Camila is twisting the end of her long brown hair again.

"You may not have enough time to whip up the perfect science stunt," says Grace. "Don't you think sticking to the plan will make things less dicey?"

"Our plans are just to hand out campaign swag."

Camila beams and snaps a finger. "Ooo, maybe you can hand them out in your Galaxy Girl costume!"

Grace points to Camila. "That could be fun. And it definitely shows personality." She grins. "And you know what? One thing on voters' wish lists is that the library carry more graphic novels and comic book series like Galaxy Girl."

I have to admit it. "That is a cute idea," I say. "But I don't think that alone is strong enough to stand up to Mason's caricatures."

Grace's sigh has a here-we-go-again flavor to it.

"This is Spirit Week, when everyone is extra pumped about school pride," I argue. "It's the perfect time to give them something extra that will turn heads."

"That sounds great, but it's also a risk when we're already doing damage control," warns Grace.

My eyes bright and my hands wildly gesturing in the air, I'm being as theatrical as Sam taught me. Without realizing it, I've dialed up my personality to prove this point to my concerned friends. "But isn't that what voters said they like most about me? That I'm a risk taker?"

Grace nods. "Just be careful not to go over the top with this. You have the town hall portion to get through after."

"I won't," I promise, and I plan not to break it.

Chapter 13

I carefully snap my phone into my tripod and press record. I walk a few paces backward, keeping myself in view. "This is it," I announce, beginning my video diary. "Spirit Day is happening after lunch today, and sure, I'm nervous. But I'm excited because I feel like it's a new day full of possibilities. I'm ready to shake things up by—*you guys!*"

In that moment, Cosmo and Rocket bound into my room and knock right into my desk, toppling my cell phone.

"Ugh, you'd think you would save all that energy for the long walk you're about to have," I say. It's pretty funny how goofy they're acting, so it's hard not to crack up. After I've had a good laugh, I continue recording.

"As I was saying—oh, wait, a video call is coming through!"

"Is this good timing?" Sam's face pops up on my screen. "I knew you'd be leaving a little earlier with your dad, so I'm glad I caught you."

"Yup," I tell Sam. "Big day."

"Yes. And I don't want to throw you off, but I wanted to share something that worked for me when I was a nervous wreck before the musical."

"Okay," I say, my eyes wide with curiosity.

Sam looks at me intently and says slowly, "One healthy shake."

"Huh?"

Sam puts down her phone, and steps back from it so that I can see her from head to toe. Next she starts wiggling her arms and legs like they're cooked spaghetti. She kinda looks like those dancing car dealer inflatables, out of control but in a fun way.

I throw my head back and crack up. "Sam, if I did that, I'd have an even bigger headache than I do now."

"C'mon, an extra mood boost couldn't hurt," she says. "Shake everything but your head if that helps!"

She sounds so sure that this will work, I start believing her, too.

"Fine." I sit my tripod on the desk again, take a few steps back, and do the Sam shake. My arms, hips, and legs wiggling nonstop actually feels fun. Cosmo and Rocket start wagging their tails and running around my kicking feet.

Sam is laughing at the whole scene. "That's good!"

After I finish, I feel a little giddy. "Thanks for the tip!"

"You're welcome. Can't wait to stop by your booth today!"

I feel warm and fuzzy knowing my bestie will be close by today. "Aw, you're the best, Sam," I say sincerely.

Again, it strikes me how super grateful I am to have friends like Sam, Grace, and Camila. When I notice the time, I forget about the video journal and head out front to my dad's car.

By the time Dad pulls up in front of JFK Middle fifteen minutes later, the school is glowing thanks to the light from the morning sun.

"Welp, here goes," I say as I reach for the car door release.

Marie leans her noggin against the front passenger seat's headrest. "Then . . . go," she says impatiently.

"Good luck today, sweetie!" Dad calls out as I step out of the car.

"Yeah, good luck!" Marie's friend Diya calls out.

"Aren't you going to wish your little sister good luck?" Dad asks Marie.

"She knows she's got this," Marie says with pride. "Do your thing, Hope!"

I smile and give them a little wave, even though my hands are full balancing everything I'm carrying.

I'm still smiling when I arrive at our assigned booth on the home field. No one else is here. Most people are setting up much later, but I'm too nervous to wait. When Grace found out that the field would be open for setup early, I told her I'd get here first thing in the morning.

Grace has to watch her kid siblings until their school bus arrives, so she won't be able to swing by the booth until later. In the meantime, I can use the peace and quiet to organize my experiment.

I pull out my printed, Grace-approved signs, comically decorated with elephant emojis, announcing: *BIG news! Have you HERD? Sixth Graders Rock! DON'T FORGET—vote for Hope! Thanks a TON!*

Satisfied with phase one of the booth setup, I head off to my morning classes.

"You look great!" Sam shouts so loud, a few people at nearby booths almost get whiplash. But it draws them over.

Yup. I'm in full Galaxy Girl costume and I only feel slightly, not fully, awkward wearing it. That's because so much of the student body is wearing school spirit gear or face paint. And one of the older candidates is wearing a tiger PJ onesie. I'm in good company.

Having Sam here in the first hour has attracted more voters over than I would have, even if I hadn't worn my Galaxy Girl costume. The girl just has that kind of magnetism. She should be a

study chapter on magnetic fields in my physics textbook!

"Hi, have you met this sixth-grade presidential hopeful?" Sam asks the whiplash crew when they arrive at our booth.

"Hello." I smile and pass out the pretty buttons and temporary tattoos Grace has arranged on our table. "Don't miss my science stunt coming up in a few."

"Look at you, Madame President-to-Be," gushes Lacy. "Let's get a pic of you with your campaign manager."

I spot Grace chatting to voters and logging in poll answers into her tablet and wave her over.

After we snap a pic, Camila, Charlie, and Golda are back from passing out flyers to draw people to my science experiment.

"Looks like we'll get a nice crowd," says Grace. "But it's not too late to opt for some dartboard fun instead. It's pretty busy in this corridor, so just wondering if you'll have enough room to do what you have to do?"

Grace is giving me a way out, but I don't take it.

"No need to worry, I got this," I say, echoing

Marie's earlier words. "It'll be fine."

"If you say so," says Grace like she knows better. I almost roll my eyes. *Does she have be so careful all the time?*

Our booth is in the perfect corner for what I have planned. It's close enough to the passing foot traffic, but tucked away enough to pull off my surprise stunt. I only wish we didn't get a spot so close to the JFK tiger mascot. Whoever's in the costume must be a gymnast—so many top-grade flips! They're giving me way too much competition for attention.

As the crowd my friends pulled starts to gather a few minutes later, I recognize the kids who felt tricked by my campaign message. They're the ones with doubting pouts on their faces. More than ever, I want to make a positive impression on everyone. Science is my superpower, so I hope I can use it to prove I'm no phony.

"Are you ready?" Grace asks.

I nod. Grace's reassuring pat on my shoulder reminds me she's in my corner, even though I am veering a little off course.

"Thanks, Grace."

In the crowd, I see Sam and Camila give me a thumbs-up and it makes me feel better. Henry's there, too. He gives me a little wave and I smile.

It's showtime.

Just then, the mascot ramps up their exhibition. My experiment could be in danger of getting upstaged. Eager to win back the crowd, I begin my science show instead of waiting for the tiger's flippy spectacle to be over. Who knows how long it will last, and there's not much time before the town hall starts. My hands move quickly as I prep the kit.

"Thank you all for coming to our Vote for Hope booth!" I announce in my best Sam-trained stage voice. "And now, something fun for JFK Spirit Day that incorporates my favorite subject—science. I hope you all enjoy."

I look at the crowd and make sure I have everyone's attention before I begin pouring the reaction solution into the giant test tube. Just when I've almost reached the amount the formula calls for, the roar of the mascot-mesmerized crowd startles me and I spill a little extra solution by accident. You'd think this crowd has never seen a tiger mascot do a split before!

"Oops," I say to myself, worried I've ruined the experiment. *What if the fun chemical reaction I'm hoping for doesn't happen?* The solution in the test tube doesn't seem to be reacting quickly enough.

But there's no harm done. Within seconds, out pours the most spectacular "elephant-sized toothpaste" foam ever, as expected. It keeps growing until it can safely be characterized as ginormous. And best of all, it's dyed maroon and yellow—JFK Middle's school colors!

People cheer and take pics, and some chuckle as they figure out the puns in my campaign signs. I'm happy with the fun results and the reactions, but I'm a little bit concerned that the foam is only spreading and growing taller. It now covers the area in front of our booth and crawls closer to the crowd.

Some people jump back to save their shoes from getting covered in the stuff. Others are so focused on the mascot's show that the foam creeps up to their feet before they have the chance to step back.

That's when all the oohs and aahs quickly turn into oh nos! The tiger is in the middle of multiple flips and doesn't realize that they're headed right for the foam.

"Wait! Stop!" I shout, running toward the tiger with my Galaxy Girl costume flapping behind me. I jump up and down and wave my arms over my head. Maybe the person in the suit can't hear me through the huge tiger head, because the flips keep on coming. I dive out of the way and watch helplessly as the tiger's paws slip on a knee-high pile of elephant toothpaste.

Everyone's mouths hang open and eyes go wide as we watch the tiger's legs do air bicycle kicks in slow motion as the mascot tries their hardest not to fall—the foam is getting close to swallowing them whole! The entire scene suddenly looks like some chaotic nature show where the tiger and "elephant" tussle it out. But thankfully, because of the mascot's nimble moves, he or she sticks the landing with style.

Whew!

The crowd cheers for the mascot while Grace rushes off to find towels. I dart over to see if they need any assistance climbing out of the foam lake, but the tiger declines when I offer my hand.

The tiger waves to everyone and accepts a few pats on the back and compliments. I'm eager to see what Olympic gymnast JFK Middle chose to wear this costume. But as the mystery person inside removes the tiger head, I pretty much want to dive back into the goo.

It's Connor, and surprise—he's not happy with me.

Chapter 14

"**D**on't come near me!" Connor shouts, holding out a furry paw.

"Connor, I—I am so, so sorry," I call out from a short distance. "I overshot the reaction solution a little. I did not expect the foam to get that big."

Connor's jaw tightens in reply, and I could swear I hear him growl. "You tried to take down the JFK Tiger, but it didn't work!"

"You tell her!" someone shouts. Connor's fury is drawing a small crowd. But this was an accident, and I won't let him make me out to be the bad guy.

"No," I say firmly. "I respect what our mascot stands for and I would never—"

"What are you going to do next—aim a slingshot at a bald eagle? Set a bear trap for a panda?"

A few people cackle and cheer for Connor.

Grace is already back with towels from the nearby locker room. She gives Connor a few before he storms away with his new fan club in tow.

"I ran into Henry, and he volunteered to find the custodian and see if they can bring a water vac to clean up the rest of the foam," she says.

"Thanks," I whisper in a daze. That's so kind of Henry. But gosh, at a time like this, why am I busy hoping Henry didn't witness my epic fail?

Grace hands me a spare towel. "Just focus on getting cleaned up as best you can. The town hall is about to start."

Grace turns to the crowd and, like the amazing campaign manager she is, directs everyone's prying eyes away from me.

Her arms gesture to the central area of the field. "We appreciate you coming. Please make your way to . . . ," she says, her voice trailing as she walks farther from me.

Charlie and Golda are busy securing the perimeter of the foam so no one walks through and risks slipping. But a few pranksters sneak in and grab armfuls of foam to play and take selfies with.

For a split second, I'm confused about why Grace handed me a towel. And then I look down at my outfit. Globs of gooey maroon foam cling to my costume and leggings and even my bare arms.

No-no-no. I have to speak in front of a huge crowd looking like I was spewed from the planet Goop? *Right now?*

"Oh, great," I groan.

It's bad enough I'm nervous, but now I'm nervous *and* yucky, and there's not enough time for me to go change in the locker room before the town hall like we planned.

The rest of my friends are by my side in a hurry,

offering me their phones as a mirror and helping me wipe off the maroon-and-yellow goo.

"Aargh, it's even in my hair?" I screech, catching my reflection in Sam's smartphone screen. "This is a disaster."

"Nothing that can't be wiped off in seconds," says Sam, using a napkin to dust a stray piece of goo off my shoulder. "See?"

I knew the foam would be elephant-sized, and I wanted it because of the wow factor that brings. But my formula goof definitely went overboard. I should have factored in the unpredictable movements of crowds and people dressed as tigers.

"The whole presentation was actually super entertaining," says ever-positive Lacy.

"Gnarly science show, Hope!" a passerby yells.

Lacy smiles at me. "You see?"

"The good news is you made an impression," Camila says.

Sam angles her phone screen at me as I wipe the gunk out of my hair.

"At this time, we'd like to invite to the stage presidential and vice presidential candidates for student council and sixth grade," an announcer calls out on the field's loudspeaker system.

It's time to face the voters. Grace is back, and she walks me over to the soundstage set up in the center of the athletic field.

"Remember, stick to the sixth-grade appreciation message and the tips you worked on with Sam and you'll be fine," she says. "As long as you speak from the heart, there's no need to worry about anything else."

We cross the track and field lanes onto the grassy pitch together, but I climb the stage steps alone. The first person I see at the top of the stairs is Milo, gesturing for me to take the vacant spot next to him, sharing his microphone stand. Mason and one of the sixth-grade VP candidates are standing at the mic neighboring ours, with a handful of other candidates at mic stands farther down the row. Sitting at the podium is our moderator, an older teacher I've seen around school.

I take a deep breath and finally look at the audience. The stage faces one side of the field's tall row of crowded bleachers. An audience of students in school colors waves pom-poms or holds up campaign signs. There are two mics set up on the track at the bottom of the bleachers, and there are already short lines forming behind them. I can't help but get wrapped up in the excitement in the air. It's cool seeing everyone showing school spirit and celebrating our school.

I get ready for whatever comes my way as the first student asks a question.

"To the student council presidential candidates," says a boy who looks like he could be in seventh or eighth grade. "What experiences prepared you to run for top office?"

Thank goodness most of the questions kids ask are directed at Milo and the other student council candidates. I get to hear Milo's thoughtful answers up close, without having to humiliate myself by hiding behind trash cans. The guy is relatable, and genuine. Of course, he doesn't have all the answers, but he admits it when he doesn't know something, and he promises to learn more about whatever knowledge he's missing.

"We only have time for three more questions," says the moderator.

I'm beginning to think I'll get away with not having to speak at all when a girl with long braids steps up to one of the mics next. "This is for the sixth-grade candidates," she says. "Can you each tell us a little about you and why you're running for office?"

This is it.

"Why don't we start with the vice president candidates and go down the line?" suggests the moderator. That means I'll go last. My heart is pounding so loud, I can barely hear the VP candidates' answers. *Deep breath in. And let it all out. In. And out.* I get my breathing under control in time to listen to Mason speak.

He lets him arms hang at his sides as he steps closer to the mic. But as he addresses the crowd, he seems to make eye contact with every person in the bleachers, and his voice sounds calm and clear.

"Hi, I'm Mason Taylor, and I'm running for sixth-grade president. I've always been interested in playing fair and playing by the rules. When I see something wrong, I'm not afraid to call it out. You can count on me to speak up for others when needed. And you don't have to worry about any confusing campaign messages with me. Everyone knows where *I* stand because I'm clear and to the point. I think we're all in this together, so if elected, feel free to approach me anytime, and we can discuss *realistic* ways to address your concerns."

The Vote for Mason section in the bleachers stands up and makes some noise and my face grows hot. Mason is clear, all right: He was shading me in his speech. I can't bring myself to look at my opponent as I begin my own statement, Grace's pep talk echoing in my mind.

I clear my throat. "Hi, I'm Hope Roberts, and I'm running for sixth-grade class president," I begin. Hearing my voice on the speakers gives me a confidence boost, and I find my voice getting stronger as I go on. "I'm not only interested in speaking *for* others. That's because I believe everyone has power in *their own* voice, and I want to encourage them to use it. I think we each make a difference—not just those of us up here running for office. And if I'm elected, I plan to work with sixth graders to let them know their voice matters and that they're equal and valued members of the JFK Middle community. Thank you."

I hear a few cheers from the bleachers, but mostly from where my friends are sitting.

"This is a question for Hope Roberts," booms the next voter's voice. I look into the crowd to see Connor at the mic.

Oh no.

"What do you say to people tagging your campaign *false Hope* and accusing you of making empty promises?" asks Connor. He doesn't even bother to hide his smirk as his new devotees start chanting "False Hope! False Hope!" A few people in the crowd join in, just for the fun of it.

This can't be happening. The chants are growing louder, and I feel wobbly from the knees up.

"That's enough," says the moderator in a stern voice. "Let's be respectful."

The jeering stops, but Connor stands there waiting for my answer.

My heart racing, I'm totally stalling as I mess

with the mic stand, raising and lowering it as I try to think up an answer. Then I bump my forehead against the mic. Milo reaches over to help me, but I adjust the stand myself before he gets the chance.

"My campaign messages weren't meant to be promises," I begin. "I can't grant wishes, no matter how much I'd love to. My posters were just intended to inspire and encourage sixth graders to dream big," I say, hoping I managed to get my point across.

"Mason Taylor, did you make any campaign promises?"

How did Connor get to ask a follow-up question when no one else could? *I guess that's one perk of being the school mascot.*

"No, I did not make any campaign promises, because I studied the student government guidebook, and I learned the responsibilities and limits of the sixth-grade class president."

Connor is addressing Mason but is looking solidly at me. "Thank you, Mason."

Burn received.

Connor's followers start up again, this time drowning out the moderator's reprimand. "False Hope! False Hope!"

I'm looking down at my damp, discolored leggings, when I hear a familiar voice at the mic.

"My question is for the audience." Chloe's friendly voice slices through the rowdy crowd. "Is this how we show school spirit? Because last I checked, Hope Roberts was a JFK tiger, too. And by the way, if you love to chant, we could totally use you at the next JV volleyball game." The jeers turn into cheers followed by a respectful silence. Chloe has everyone's attention. "I've read the student government handbook, too—it's something we civics club kids do for fun." The crowd chuckles. "And yes, I understand there are limits to what even the student council president can do. But when it comes to helping or inspiring a fellow student, my take is that there are no limits.

"So maybe we can find some solutions together, like planning a fund-raiser for a new volleyball net or building a database of volunteers we can tap into. Let's start thinking about what we admire about the different ways everyone campaigned. It was pretty cool to see the candidates motivate their classmates and spark their imaginations with the *messages* they put out. What's really important is that we support each other's goals, no matter who wins the election, because they benefit us all."

The applause Chloe receives for her "question" is so heartwarming, I feel a sense of unity with the audience as I clap along.

"Thank you for that," the moderator answers her. "Can we ask what your name is?"

Chloe stands in place and gives a slight smile.

"I'm Chloe Farzan, and I'm in the sixth grade."

Heads turn to Chloe, and even though she flinches at the sudden focus on her, she recovers and walks back to her seat with her usual thoughtful vibe.

After the event is over, the candidates all shake hands before we leave the stage.

"I really liked your speech," says Milo. "I hope you're proud of yourself."

Milo reaches out for a handshake, and for once, it's just a simple straightforward one.

"Thank you," I tell him. He nods, unaware that I'm also thanking him for sparing me from his elaborate high fives. I definitely don't feel high-energy enough right now to get through one of those.

When I step off the stage, Sam, Camila, and Lacy wrap me up in a group hug.

"Grace ran over to take exit polls. She said for you to head home and you'd chat later."

I feel weird leaving before seeing Grace, but right now all I want to do is get cleaned up. Despite what Milo said and Chloe's inspiring words, I leave the field feeling like I have some serious rethinking to do before election day.

Chapter 15

My family doesn't have to ask how today went. They can read it on my face when I get home—and on my messy costume.

After I've showered and changed, Mom and my pups come into my room to check up on me. Cosmo and Rocket let me pet them for a little while before they zip across my room to monitor the activity out the window.

"Hey, you can invite your friends over if you'd like," Mom suggests gently.

"They're all busy," I say, plopping down on the bed. I reach for my planet Mars pillow and hug it tight. What I don't tell my mom is that I haven't heard from Grace yet. No doubt, the poll results she collected are probably coming to the same hard truth I am: I torpedoed my campaign today.

I have to discuss things with Grace, but the way I feel now, I'd be happy not to talk about the day's events with anyone ever again.

Mom sits next to me and rubs my back. "You don't have to tell us what happened today until you're ready," she says. Sometimes I wonder if she's a mind reader. "But your dad and I just want you to know we are proud of you, no matter what."

I puff and drop my head. "Even if I'm not so sure I want to do this anymore?"

Mom reaches out and lifts my chin. "Are you sure this isn't because you had one bad day?"

My eyes meet hers. "It's not just about today— which I will not discuss." It's tough, but I manage not to mentally play back the embarrassing highlights from town hall. "The campaign has been getting kind of overwhelming for a while now."

My mom nods in understanding. "Well, maybe it would help to remind yourself why you decided to run in the first place."

"I wanted to make my mark at JFK Middle, the

way you and Marie did," I admit. "And I wanted to help other people make their marks, too."

"From where I sit, it seems you've already been doing that through science club and the animal shelter fund-raiser."

Hmm . . . I never thought about it that way. "I guess?"

"So it's okay if running for president isn't a good fit for you," she says. "Being a class officer is a huge commitment and a lot of responsibility. If you win the election, it wouldn't be fair to your classmates for you to pull out then."

I release the Mars pillow from my hug and rest it comfortably on my lap.

Mom moves a few of my curly strands away from my eye. "The decision is yours to make," she says. "I'm sure you'll make the right one—whatever it is."

On her way out, Mom kisses my forehead and reminds me about family movie night.

When I take my position on the couch a little while later, not even tough-love Marie pushes me to share. Instead, my family just lets me pick the snack.

During the movie, I send out a quick text to Grace.

Hey, thank you for everything today. Weekend meetup? I need to talk to you. Thinking about dropping out of the race.

As busy as I know Grace is with her spreadsheets and endless babysitting duties, she responds almost right away.

Let's talk tomorrow afternoon.

I don't know if it's because of relief or worry, but I fall asleep during the movie, right there on the couch.

♡ ☑ ☆

The next morning, my dad drives me and the dogs to my favorite seaside park. He knows being outside near the ocean breeze always cheers me up. It perks up Cosmo and Rocket, too. They barely give me a chance to make it to the dog release area before they're off and running. Once they're safely gated, I find a nearby bench where I can watch them.

"Chloe?" I say to the girl already seated on the bench.

Chloe looks up from her journal writing and smiles back at me.

"It's so cool running into you here," I tell her. "You were amazing at the town hall. Marie told me that everyone's been sharing that video of your speech online. It's kinda gone JFK viral!"

She grins. "Funny enough, a lot of people stopped me to talk afterward. And my phone's been blowing up with messages today."

"I'm not surprised. You're a rock star! Thank you for being the voice of reason."

"I said those things because they were the truth," she says with a shrug. "I definitely didn't expect this reaction, though. I'm the world's biggest intro-vert, so don't expect it to happen again!" Chloe says with a smile, mostly joking.

I give her a grateful smile. "Well, it takes a spe-cial person to do what you did—and by that, I mean recruiting the JV volleyball team's new cheer section!"

Chloe pumps her fist in victory, and we both crack up and high-five each other.

I glance over at what Cosmo and Rocket are up to. Someone made the mistake of leaving behind their half-eaten banana and the seagulls are flock-ing. Cosmo and Rocket couldn't be happier about this. I watch them zip after their feathered foes before bringing my attention back to Chloe and her journal.

"So, were you jotting down more of your ideas?"

"No, this time I was doing some creative writing," she says.

I'm curious. "Really? Are you writing a book or something?"

"Poetry," she replies. "It's just a rough draft, but if you promise not to judge, you can have a look."

I take the journal and a seat next to her. An

ocean breeze whips through and turns the pages. I
flip back to the poem and pin down
the fluttering pages.

A word
A voice
An act
A choice
Complain
Rejoice
Off track
On course
The choice is yours.

"Whoa, this is beautiful and
so smart," I say with a dreamy
sigh after I finish reading.
"JFK Middle needs to hear more voices like
yours."

"Aw, thank you," she says humbly. "JFK needs
your voice, too."

I nod slowly. "Yeah, it does—but maybe not as a
candidate," I confess.

Chloe grimaces like she has a tummy ache.

"Disappointed?" I ask her.

"I'm just so sorry to hear that," Chloe says right

away. "But how could I be disappointed in someone like you? You know that you need to do what's best for you—even if it's not easy. And with your brain and big heart, you'll still be an important member of the JFK community, even if you're not class president."

"There you go, spouting words of wisdom again!" I say with a big smile. "I should have hired you as my campaign speech writer. With your leadership skills and student government knowledge—"

Wait. *Leadership skills. Student government knowledge.*

The thought is still swirling in my mind, and I guess I'm still staring because Chloe asks, "What is it?"

"Oh, it's nothing. I was just imagining you running for office," I say.

Chloe leans away and takes in a different angle of me, which makes us both chuckle. "You have a vivid imagination," she says.

"Well, if you ever find *yourself* thinking about it, you should talk to my campaign manager, Grace," I suggest. "She's coming over later today if you want to swing by. Totally no pressure about committing to anything."

Chloe sits perfectly still as the thought marinates. "But isn't it too late to join the race?"

"Well . . . there *is* a special exception," I explain. "Late entries are allowed only if the race has an uncontested opponent." Funny how much I learned when I finally got around to reading the student government handbook. "And all the worries about being an introvert shouldn't stop you—if that's what you're worried about," I say. "I know some girls who could teach you a few pointers about stage presence and all that. You'd be fine."

Chloe nods thoughtfully. "Huh. I guess I have some thinking to do," she says.

Just as I hand her back her open journal, another gust of wind flips Chloe's pages, rapid-fire, and out comes a loose sheet of paper. We both jump up to grab it before it goes farther down the beach. I catch it and get a glimpse of what's expertly scribbled on the paper when I hand it to Chloe.

"Is that a drawing of you?" I ask, impressed.

"It's my caricature," she says.

"Mason Taylor," we both say at the same time and grin.

Chloe's eyes meet mine. "I hope you know you still had my vote, but I just had to. He's so good."

"My biggest regret from Spirit Day is not making it to his booth," I confess.

It's not long before we dissolve into laughter. Yesterday was hard, but today is already looking a lot brighter.

Chapter 16

I've just set out three glasses of water at the small table by our pool when Grace steps into my back-yard. I hadn't even heard the bell.

"How are you?" Grace and I ask each other at the same time.

When we both laugh, I can feel the tension between us melting. We plop down on the cushioned chairs, clearly exhausted from holding in all these feelings.

"I should be asking *you* how *you're* doing," I say.

"No, I should be asking you," answers Grace. "I wanted to give you some space to let everything that happened at Spirit Day sink in."

I do my *Can you believe it?* face. "And I wanted to give *you* some space because I know that I let you down," I say.

Grace leans forward and rests an elbow on the table. "Why do you always think I'll be mad or disappointed in you?"

"Well, I went against your campaign advice and went all wish-list warrior on everyone," I say. Now my own elbows are also on the table, supporting my double facepalm.

"Hope, I'm here to advise you, but it's your campaign. So it's totally up to you to take that advice or not," says Grace, like the sensible person she is. "Yes, it can be frustrating when you do your own thing, but I try not to take it personally. It's a part of the job."

I touch my hand to my heart and let out a huge sigh of relief.

"Grace, honestly, I'm so glad our friendship could stand up to all the wackiness of a middle school election," I say.

"And all the wackiness of a passionate, headstrong candidate," says Grace, letting out a cackle.

"Fair enough," I say, shrugging.

Grace corrects herself. "Or should I say *former* candidate?"

I take a deep breath and nod.

Grace drops her head. "Are you sure? Because I think you'd be great in office. You're amazing at getting people to care or act or get involved."

Like Miss MVP Emma, I'm touched to hear someone is rooting for me. "Really?"

"Yes. It's like you give a purpose to everything you do, and that's really special."

"Wow. I don't know if I ever realized you see me that way."

"A lot of us do," she says. "But if you're sure about your decision, I understand."

"Thanks, Grace," I say, relieved. "Dropping out doesn't mean I'm not proud of the work we did.

Having you by my side made me feel a lot braver and a whole lot more wish-granty than I actually am."

"Is 'wish-granty' even a word?" Grace teases with a slight smile.

I slap the table like I mean business. "I'll see what I can do to get the powers that be to make it one."

"Very funny."

My phone pings. It's Chloe saying she's just been dropped off at my house.

"Chloe is here!" I announce. "She's considering running for class president in my place, and she wants to talk it over with us."

"The now-famous Chloe Farzan?" asks Grace, rising out of her seat. "That's amazing! The people I polled after the town hall couldn't stop talking about her speech."

I laugh. "Good to see you're totally over my dropping out of the race."

"Why are you bringing up old news?" Grace asks with a mischievous smirk.

We both cackle so hard, when Chloe walks out of the house, she can't help but crack up, too.

We manage to get serious enough to talk what-ifs with Chloe. Grace whips up a quick scenario of how she would manage Chloe's late-start campaign.

"We'd have a lot of ground to cover in a short amount of time, but I think you'd have a fair shot at winning," says Grace, pointing at her graphs and latest polls.

Chloe leans back in her seat, arms splayed, her face to the sky, and says, "This doesn't sound so out of my league anymore."

"If anyone can do it, you can!" I tell her.

Grace and I play with Cosmo and Rocket to give

Chloe some space to think. She walks away to call her parents to discuss things with them. It's hard to tell which way the conversation is going from the other side of the yard, but when she takes a seat at our table, she's got a huge smile on her face.

"Okay, I'm in," Chloe says.

Grace and I jump out of our seats and cheer!

Chloe jumps up, too, and high-fives us. "Let's do this!"

Chloe agrees to meet us at the makers' space

first thing Monday morning. Next, I text Sam, and she's on board to meet Chloe then, too.

I may not have been the best candidate for sixth-grade class president, but now that I found the girl who is, I am going to do everything I can to help her win.

♡☑☆

After Grace leaves, I head to my room to record a video. But the difference with this recording is that it isn't just for me. I plan to share it with the student government advisor, Ms. Reimer.

According to the student government handbook, a candidate must submit a letter of withdrawal if they drop out of the race. But a video is more my style.

"My name is Hope Roberts, and effective immediately, I am withdrawing from the sixth-grade class presidential race. Thank you to all who inspired me and cheered me on. I made a few mistakes, and I've disappointed some, but as Einstein once said, 'A person who never made a mistake never tried something new.' I would not change this experience for the world. I got to meet so many people, and I've learned that every single one of us has a role to play at JFK Middle. Today, I'm willing to accept that mine is not as class president. But I can't wait to contribute to our school in my own unique way. Together, let's all keep putting the 'spirit' in Spirit Day and the 'rawr' in the JFK Tiger."

After I send the video to Ms. Reimer, I feel light as air.

Chapter 17

First thing Monday morning, I arrive at the makers' space to find Chloe, Grace, and Sam already there. We got Ms. Reimer's official approval, so now this campaign is in full swing. One airy corner has already become the Chloe Farzan campaign headquarters. The sunlight beaming through the large window onto the oversized, high-back swivel seats make it the perfect nook for brainstorming.

"Hot off the press!" I shout as I walk to the center table and place down the posters I've printed on recycled paper. The girls race over to check out the finished product.

We squeal over Archie's illustration of Chloe, in Alice in Wonderland's iconic blue dress, standing next to the tardy rabbit who holds up his pocket watch. The slogan says, *It's not too late to pick the right candidate: Vote Chloe Farzan.*

"I love it!" says Grace.

I'm so happy to see Grace and Chloe hitting it off super well. The two of them are clearly on the same page. I can't believe how much they make a data-driven, strategy-loving duo, except that Chloe is definitely more analog while Grace is more digital.

Sam and Chloe have obviously bonded, too.

"You know, Chloe," says Sam. "Your poems would make great acting monologues."

Watching my oldest friend help prep my newest friend for this exciting role is special. Chloe is a natural leader, and after her town hall speech, so many people know they can trust her to get things done. In the short time I've known her, she's opened my eyes to so much. I'm excited for the rest of the school to see all she has to offer.

Before we head to class, Grace sits us down and delivers our game plan.

"Chloe's done most of the legwork, so we're ready to hit the ground running," she says.

Chloe sits forward in her chair and looks each of us in the eyes. "Hope's sixth-grade appreciation work is inspiring me to take my message to another level. I will work hard to make sure overlooked kids don't stay invisible. They are just as important to JFK Middle and to sixth grade as anyone else."

"That's beautiful," says Sam.

"Hope," Chloe says. "I would love if you would canvass the school with me. That way you can show me some of your favorite spots to meet voters."

"Of course," I say, willing to do anything she

needs. I try to ignore the feeling that my presence on the campaign trail could hurt her standings. Plus, I'm also worried about running into the people I've disappointed.

During study period, once Chloe and I start making the rounds, it isn't long before my past comes calling.

"Hope Roberts?" a voice echoes down the hall outside the library. *Oh no, here we go.*

I turn to see Emma and her teammates.

"Hey!" Chloe and I exclaim. I wonder if they're as excited to see us. Even though they got a shout-out during Spirit Week, they haven't received any *real* perks from my campaign—most especially, a brand-new volleyball net.

"Hope," barks Emma. Chloe and I reach for each other's hands. "One day I'd love to teach you how to *really* serve." Emma beams that dimpled smile of hers.

Everyone cracks up, and I puff out a huge sigh of relief.

"Yes, please." I grin. "But for now, would you guys want to be in a selfie with Chloe, our new presidential candidate?"

"Let's do it!" says Emma, wrapping her long arms around her teammates and getting into position.

It's cool that I can use my new familiarity with kids to boost support for Chloe. I snap a few pics using Chloe's selfie stick before we break apart and go our separate ways.

Exchanges like these—both positive and negative—play out again and again over the next few days. But by the middle of the week, I'm feeling relieved the drama surrounding me is toning down. Kids start to move on from the elephant toothpaste

goof and the gotcha question at the town hall. And I have this new confidence and way less hesitation about going up and speaking to other sixth graders I don't know.

But the best surprise of all is that people recognize Chloe and remember what she said during the Spirit Day town hall. Her popularity seems to have continued to build from there.

I just hope we're doing enough to keep that going.

♡ ☑ ☆

On the morning of election day, all our friends get together at the makers' space headquarters for the last time. Grace has conducted four polls in the last four days. She's reported good and not so great news with each one, and we brace ourselves for her final findings.

"Mason is edging out Chloe by a few points, but maybe we can get one last push today," reports Grace.

"How do you suggest we do that?" Camila asks.

Grace shrugs and shakes her head. "The best we can do now is talk Chloe up until the minute we go to the polls."

Chloe checks the time on her phone. "Which is now," she says.

We all gather our things, but before we start for the voting booths in the gym, Chloe stops us.

"Hey, guys. I just want to thank you from the bottom of my heart. What we've done together here was beyond anything I imagined. I'm so glad Hope and Grace and I booked the same study room. It's incredible where that has led me and I'm grateful, no matter who wins today."

"Oh, Chloe." Sam is choked up and holding back tears. Sniffing, she reaches for tissues in her back pocket, but pulls out her phone instead. "I—oh, wait a minute."

"Really, Sam?" I ask teasingly. "That can't wait?"

But Sam's eyes are glued to her screen and she

starts to wildly flap a hand in the air. "OMG, guys! Archie texted me and said that Milo just officially endorsed Chloe for sixth-grade class president!"

"No. Way," deadpans Chloe.

Grace and I high-five each other, but I keep the handshake going like Milo would.

Poll numbers and endorsements are important, but not as important as actually voting. So, not wanting to put the cart before the horse, we calmly enter the gym. Lined along three walls are make-shift booths that are really just tables separated into walled cubicles. There are only about twenty of them, so if we didn't get here early enough, there would surely be a wait.

When it's my turn, I am given a ballot and directed to a corner desk to fill it out. I have a seat and look over all the sixth-grade and student council candidates that are listed. It's weird to think my own name was almost an option.

Shaking off any regrets or doubts, it feels great to proudly cast my ballot for all of the different positions—including for Chloe and Milo.

♡ ☑ ☆

After lunch almost every sixth grader is hanging out in the makers' space, waiting to hear the results.

"How are you feeling?" I ask Chloe when I spot her sitting in one corner, writing in her journal. Grace is next to her, quietly tapping away on her tablet.

Chloe shrugs. "Whatever happens, I did my best."

I nod, loving her attitude.

"Guys, the results are coming in," Camila shushes us from across the room.

Ms. Reimer's voice is in surround sound, piping through the PA system loud and clear, as she rattles off the names of elected candidates. She begins with the eighth-grade winners. We wait for what feels like forever for the sixth-grade results.

Chloe's friends stand close by, trying not to act as nervous as they look. I'm pretty sure mine isn't the only tummy churning as we sit or pace or stand patiently.

And then it's finally time.

"The sixth grade's new class president is . . . Chloe Farzan!" Ms. Reimer finally announces.

"I did it!" Chloe jumps up and down and squeals. "*We* did it!"

We erupt in cheers.

"This is amazing!" shouts Chloe, her hands on her cheeks in disbelief.

It's such a sweet feeling. I throw my arms around her and give her a squeeze as Ms. Reimer's voice drones on with the student council results. "Congratulations!"

When I break away from Chloe, Camila takes my hand and rushes me closer to the PA speaker. "Didn't you hear?"

"Hear what?" I ask, confused.

"Community outreach officer—write-in candidate: Hope Roberts," says Sam breathlessly.

"Congratulations to you, too," Camila squeals.

My eyes bug out and I cover my mouth with one hand. "No way!" I say.

"Yes, way," says Grace. "And it looks like you'll be working closely with Milo, our new student council vice president!"

"This is such a perfect role for you," says Lacy.

I shake my head. I want nothing more than to call my family and tell them the good news. But it'll be even sweeter when I tell them in person.

Chapter 18

The next week, it feels like a new energy has taken over JFK Middle. The halls are buzzing more than usual for a Monday afternoon. That's because it's inauguration day! All the elected students are gathering in the auditorium for the swearing-in ceremony. Plus, everyone is starting to talk up our sixth-grade field trip, which is just a few weeks away. Rumors are already swirling that we'll be expected to rough it in the wilderness. And word is, the older kids from science club have been invited to come to the two-day visit to the nature preserve, too.

"Hey, Hope," someone calls out. When I turn around, it's Henry.

He jogs up to me, his basketball jersey billowing when the air catches it. I hope this means he's coming to the ceremony.

"I'm heading to the auditorium, too," he says, confirming my suspicions. "Mind if I walk with you?"

It's been a while since Henry's asked me that question. It's nice to hear it again.

"Sure," I say as casually as possible. "It's nice of you to come watch everyone get sworn in."

"Yeah, it should be cool. Besides, I have more time on my hands now with the musical and the elections over." He shrugs. "By the way, I haven't had a chance to congratulate you on your win!"

"Thank you." My smile melts away when I realize what I have to do. I've chatted with so many people, you'd think this would get less awkward. But talking to Henry about it just feels different. "Uh, thanks for being so cool even though I weirded out on you during the campaigning process," I say.

"Oh, that," Henry says, looking as if he feels as awkward as I do. *What does he have to feel awkward about?*

"I was trying to do too much, and I guess I was

letting my, uh, curiosity about Milo muddy up my thinking," I continue. "I'm sorry I let it affect our friendship, because I really like our friendship."

"It's okay," says Henry, clearing his throat. "Milo has that, um, effect on some people."

I wrinkle my nose in confusion. I was trying to apologize for being so busy during the campaign, so why . . .

Wait. Does Henry *really* think I have a crush on Milo? *Is that why he's acting so nervous all of a sudden?*

I stop walking and look Henry in the eyes. "Oh, no. I don't mean I have a crush on Milo, because I totally don't. I just think he has amazing leadership skills."

"Oh. Yeah. Th—that makes total sense now," he says, rubbing the back of his neck in thought. A slow smile creeps up his lips, and Henry breaks into a cackle.

"Are you laughing at me?" I grin.

"I'm sorry, I just got an image of you crouching behind that trash can, and—" He cracks up again.

The image is just so horrible and Henry's laugh so funny that I can't help but join in as we continue to the auditorium. Before we go in, Henry stops to look at me.

"Hey, thanks for saying that about our friendship. I like our friendship, too."

I'm still smiling as I enter the auditorium and head up to the stage with the other newly elected officers of JFK Middle.

"Thanks so much for coming," Ms. Reimer says to the small audience of friends. I'm standing between Chloe and Milo, and I look around at the supportive faces of Sam, Grace, Camila, Lacy, Golda, Charlie, and Henry in the crowd. Unlike the last time I was on a stage, I feel excited rather than overwhelmed. There are no knots in my stomach, only happily fluttering butterflies.

As Ms. Reimer swears me in to my new role, I think about what my mom said and enjoy this feeling that the community outreach officer role is the right fit for me. I'm ready to serve JFK Middle in the unique ways I know how.

After the short ceremony, the auditorium clears out quickly, but I ask my friends to stay back and join me on the stage.

"This will only take a few minutes," I tell them. "I want to thank you all for your help through my short-lived campaign experience. And I'm here to say there's one campaign promise I did deliver on. From now on, JFK Middle's library will carry the entire catalog of Galaxy Girl comic books!"

"Yay!" my friends whoop.

"And to mark this special occasion," I announce, reaching behind the podium for a replica Galaxy Girl doll mounted on an engraved collector's stand, "I'd like to present Grace, a superstar campaign manager and all-around amazing friend, with this Galaxy Girl power award."

Grace freezes and her mouth forms an O before she snaps out of it and steps up to receive her trophy.

"You totally surprised me!" she says. We both laugh as she throws her arms around me.

"After my campaign, you should be used to that by now," I tease.

Grace shakes her head and shoulder-bumps me.

I wave to all my gathered friends. "Come on, let me show you all how to do the Galaxy Girl power pose."

We're all giggling as everyone copies my wide stance and lengthened spine. It's cool to see how each one of us owns the look in a unique way. Just

like Galaxy Girl, I feel ready to take on anything that comes my way—as long as I have my friends by my side. I swing my arms over my friends' shoulders, and we all walk out of the auditorium and on to our next adventure at JFK Middle.

HOPE'S TIPS

I learned so much running for class president! Now that I'm community outreach officer, it's my duty to inform everyone about the election process. Whether it's for your school elections today or for president in the future, voting is super important. It's how YOU get a say in the way your community is run! The candidates you choose can make the difference in whether the issues you care about are addressed.

Here are some tips on how to vote like a model citizen, too!

Pay attention: From the moment a candidate announces she's running for office, she'll spend every day trying to earn the public's vote. This is a good time to hear out all the candidates, ask questions, and discuss your thoughts with a friend. Remember: Elections are as much about you and your community as they are about the candidates.

Do some research: During an election season, there will be a downpour of unfamiliar glossary words. But don't let this scare you! Are you voting for someone representing your class or district? You're their "constituent." Have you told a friend who you're voting for? You've just "endorsed" that candidate! And do you remember my campaign on sixth-grade appreciation? That message was my "platform." Elections get easier to understand once you take a little mystery out of the terms.

Protect yourself: If pepperoni is your favorite pizza topping, you probably should steer clear of the candidate promising an all-pineapple-toppings cafeteria menu. This is called voting against your interests. Elected officials should represent the community they serve. They won't always tick all your must-have boxes, but your vote is a signal that you trust them to speak on your behalf and protect the matters that are important to you.

Show your support: Once you've figured out which candidate is best for you, make sure you get out there and spread the word! Campaigns are always looking for volunteers to make phone calls, pass out flyers, and knock on doors. Ask a parent if you can tag along next time they hit the streets to promote their favorite candidate!

Get to the polls: It sounds like a no-brainer, but you'd be surprised how many people forget it's Election Day or arrive at their polling location without proper ID. So, be sure you do all that's required to cast your ballot on the big day! Start by reminding your parents to check if their voter registration info is up-to-date. Voting is a privilege that so many people had to fight for. Let's honor the process and show up to rock the vote!

About the Author

Dirk Franke

ALYSSA MILANO began acting when she was only 10 years old. She has continued to work in both TV and movies since then, including hit shows like *Who's the Boss?* and *Charmed.* Alyssa is also a lifelong activist who is passionate about fighting for human rights around the world. She has been a National Ambassador for UNICEF since 2003, and she enjoys speaking to students in schools around the country about the importance of voting. She was named one of *Time* magazine's Persons of the Year in 2017 for her activism. Alyssa lives in Los Angeles with her husband and two kids. This is her first children's book series.

About the Author

Chanda Williams

DEBBIE RIGAUD is the coauthor of Alyssa Milano's Hope series and the author of *Truly Madly Royally*. She grew up in East Orange, New Jersey, and started her career writing for entertainment and teen magazines. She now lives with her husband and children in Columbus, Ohio. Find out more at debbierigaud.com.

About the Illustrator

ERIC S. KEYES is currently an animator and character designer on *The Simpsons*, having joined the show in its first season. He has worked on many other shows throughout the years, including *King of the Hill*, *The Critic*, and *Futurama*. He was also a designer and art director on Disney's *Recess*. Hope is his first time illustrating a children's series. Eric lives in Los Angeles with his wife and son.